The
MERCHANT
From
BETHLEHEM

Johan Christian

Emerald Press
Rocklin, California

The Merchant From Bethlehem

Published By
Emerald Press
Rocklin, California 95677

ISBN 0-9650369-0-1

Printed in the United States of America
First Printing

Lovingly dedicated to my dear wife.

Chapter One

Simon and Rachel walked hand in hand through the corridor of their villa which lead to the gardens of their small, but beautiful estate. They exited the dwelling through a cedar door and stepped out onto the tiled veranda. Flowing palm and date trees, along with lush green plants and blossoming desert flowers adorned the encircling grounds, while the pungent and sweet aroma of citrus fruit permeated the air. A shimmering brook coursed its way through the colorful gardens which, with its many natural waterfalls, rendered peace and tranquility to the soul.

It is here, amongst the serenity of their estate, that Simon and Rachel enjoyed walking together in the cool evening air, marveling at the splendor of the setting sun and listening to the song birds that nest high in the trees.

After their stroll, the couple rested on a dark mahogany lounge comfortably situated under one of the large, shady palm trees which Simon had planted on their estate in the city of Cyrene some twenty-five years earlier. Their eyes met and each affectionately gazed at the other.

"Time has passed so quickly," he whispered to himself as he turned to look out onto the Great Sea, the southern shore of which bordered the estate. Already it had been thirty years since the death of the Messiah, and Simon was now in his fifty-second year of life.

"Do you recall what day this is, my husband?" asked Rachel as she brushed a fallen leaf from Simon's thinning hair.

Simon ever so slowly nodded his head as he watched the gentle waves fall against the shore. "How is one to forget such memorable events?"

"Can it be possible that thirty years have passed since the week of the race?" questioned Rachel, not believing the swift passage of time. "It was not so long ago that our children played about this tree and now they have all married and begun lives of their own. I cannot believe that so many years have come and gone with such haste. It makes me feel so old."

Simon drew a deep breath and sighed heavily. How he loved the smell of the sea. "Thirty years and yet it seems as if it were but yesterday." He then turned and smiled at Rachel. "And yet it appears that time has mercifully ignored you, my love, for you are as beautiful as ever."

Rachel laughed aloud as she threw her head back into the air. "You are indeed a wonderful husband, Simon, but time has dimmed your once youthful vision."

She then stood and walked behind her husband where she began to gently massage his tired muscles. Even through his robe she could still feel the large scar which crossed his back and shoulders. "I thought it would have disappeared by now," she said.

2

Simon reached for her hand upon his shoulder. "I also had similar hopes, my dearest Rachel, and yet in a way I am pleased that the scar still remains, for it is a constant reminder of both terrible and wonderful days gone past, days which must never be forgotten."

Rachel nodded her agreement and returned to the lounge where she sat beside her husband. She nestled up against him, placing her head on his shoulder. Neither of them could revisit the past without experiencing the deepest of emotions. Simon ran his fingers through Rachel's soft, graying hair as he looked out over the sea, a gentle wind blew in his face. He strived to think back in time, approximately thirty years ago. . . .

Chapter Two

Young Simon gazed dejectedly at the hot afternoon sun which unmercifully passed overhead. He had been at the plow since early morning and his back was aching miserably. He removed the worn scarf from around his neck and wiped the stinging sweat from his brow.

He walked over to the old mule to retrieve some water, which by now had turned warm from the heat of the day. Simon removed the old, leather vessel from the pack and gulped down the tasteless liquid, but its lack of refreshing coolness did little to quench his unrelenting thirst. He wiped the excess water from his parched lips with the back of his hand and shook his head slowly back and forth in despair as he contemplated his sorrowful predicament.

Simon was not happy with his life and discouragement filled his troubled soul. His heart, however, had not always been tormented with such discontent, for if the truth were told, Simon's life had indeed been so very full of endless promise just three years earlier.

That is when he had married his beautiful Rachel, the love of his youth, and at that time he had embarked on a promising career as a merchant selling valuable wares door to door and at the local markets in his home town of Cyrene. Rachel had given birth to their daughter, Rebecca, just a year following the wedding and was now once again heavy with their second child. But with terrible suddenness, Simon's bright future had vanished, supplanted by what was to be a most dreadful ordeal.

Shortly after the wedding, Simon had suffered a life-threatening accident. A neighbor's house had caught fire in the midst of the night and Simon had rushed into the deadly inferno to save a helpless child. His attempt, although successful, brought tragedy to young Simon, for during the rescue his face and neck were badly burned and he lost the use of his right eye. Losing a portion of his vision was a fate he could have learned to live with, but sadly for Simon, a greater misfortune resulted; for the burns had caused a permanent and grotesque scarring of the right side of his face.

Since that time, Simon felt terribly self-conscious and could barely stand to look upon another human being for fear of their response. As a consequence, Simon found it difficult, if not impossible, to approach people in the marketplace or in the streets. His business suffered greatly and the task of supporting his young family became ever so arduous.

Every morning at sunrise, Simon had to force himself out of the comfort and security of his warm bed to meet another day's rejections and failures. He found himself leaving his house later and later each day and then quitting his day's work to return home, earlier and earlier in the afternoon. Some days he did not even feel like leaving the house at all, and often he would labor for only a few hours and then sit for the remainder of the day by the Great Sea, throwing bread crumbs to the hungry gulls that battled for the little food he could spare.

It was there that Simon would gaze into the waters of the calm sea, and while looking upon his mirrored image he would try to understand why such a terrible injustice had happened to him. Why now, when all seemed to be progressing so well? What horrible offense had he committed that a just God would curse him in such a repulsive manner? Often he would cover the maimed side of his face and dream of the time before the accident when his image was handsome and normal, and did not elicit pitiful stares from those who passed by.

In time, Simon's business failed. He was thus forced to abandon his dream and take employment as the sole laborer on one of the smaller farms on the outskirts of Cyrene. His reward for such service was but a meager existence and the work was back-breaking, but at least he labored in solitude and did not have to endure the presence of others.

He remained at home as much as possible, but whenever he did venture out of the security of his house, he cloaked himself in a hooded garment which covered the majority of his face. No one saw him except close family.

Simon and Rachel were both Jewish, but lived far away from the kingdom of Judah and it's capital city of Jerusalem. It was three centuries ago that their ancestors had departed their homeland of Judea and had traveled a great distance to the northern African coastal city of Cyrene, in the Cyrenaica province, to establish a settlement on the Great Sea. There, the colony had flourished through the production of wheat, oils and wool and by selling valuable wares brought in by the over-laden barges which sailed from Syracuse,

Tyre, Athens, Corinth, Alexandria and every other city of commerce that lay along the Great Sea in the days of the Roman Empire.

Simon had fallen deeply in love with Rachel while he was yet a lad, and had waited anxiously for the day when the two would be of proper age so that he might ask for her hand in marriage. When the promised day finally arrived, Simon had dressed in his best attire, though very humble raiment it was, and confidently approached Rachel's father. Simon was but eighteen years of age at the time.

There was much discussion between the two men that night, but Simon would remember only one small, but important part of their conversation; Rachel's father desired to know how Simon had planned on providing for his only daughter. Simon stood proudly before his future father-in-law and enthusiastically proclaimed his plans of becoming the most successful merchant in the city of Cyrene! Rachel, Simon assured her father, would be well cared for and have the best that the world could offer.

That was three years ago. An eternity. And during that time the dreams of his youth had been shattered. Simon stood in the midst of the barren field, the plow at his feet, sobbing like a small child, his soul ridden with fear, despair, worry and guilt. He was failing his beloved Rachel, and perhaps of greater importance, he was failing himself. And what troubled him most of all was that he had not even a notion of how to escape the prison which held his tormented soul captive.

Simon slowly opened the door to his humble, two-room dwelling and little Rebecca, upon seeing her father enter the house, ran to greet him without delay. "Father! Father!" she screamed with delight.

"Hello, my precious," said Simon as he feigned a smile and a pretended laugh. "How was your day?"

The little girl giggled as Simon lifted her into the air. "Mother taught me how to make unleavened bread

7

for the Passover!"

"She did?!"

"Uh-huh."

Simon kissed Rebecca on the cheek and held her close to him as he walked towards Rachel, who stood laboring near the fire. "Well, you must have learned to make the best bread in the entire world, for there is not a better cook to be found in all the city of Cyrene."

Rachel looked up and fondly smiled at her husband. She was indeed a beautiful young woman; barely twenty years of age. She had long, flowing brown hair with big, dark eyes and striking features. Her face, however, was fuller than normal because she carried a child. Simon approached her timidly and kissed her gently on the cheek.

"How was your day?" she softly inquired.

"Well, I suppose." His head was slightly bowed as he spoke.

"Would you like some cold water?" she asked.

Simon nodded, but said nothing. Rachel poured the water into a small goblet and placed it on the table in front of Simon, and as she did so, she bent over and kissed him on the head and tousled his hair.

Rachel loved Simon more than words could describe, and even though they were experiencing hardships, she still adored him in every way. Simon's deformity did not diminish her strong feelings for him, but it hurt her deeply to see her husband suffer so, to lose his once unbridled passion and zest for life. They seldom spoke of it, but ever since the fire, she could sense his lost confidence and wounded ego, something she completely understood, but at the same time she prayed that he would somehow find a way to rise above this challenge.

That night, as they lay in bed together, Simon turned towards the wall, away from Rachel, his back shielding him from her face and the pain he felt. Rachel, however, cuddled up to Simon and placed

8

a soft kiss on his neck.

"Do not worry," she whispered. "We will get through this. You shall see."

Simon closed his eyes and sighed heavily. "You deserve better, Rachel . . . you deserve someone . . ."

"I deserve the best," interrupted Rachel, her voice soft and quiet, yet unwavering. "I deserve you."

"You see how the people stare at us when we walk to the marketplace. It cannot be easy for you to be married to someone like me." Simon then gazed about the room. "And look at what I have been able to provide for you . . . two rooms with dirt floors."

Rachel sat up in bed and softly lifted her hand to touch Simon's face. "I do not care what other people see or think, nor do I care where we live. I love you, Simon."

She then delicately turned his face towards hers and gazed into his eyes. "And I know deep down that all shall be well . . . I have faith in you. I always have and I always will."

Simon closed his eyes. If only he could feel the same way, he thought.

Chapter Three

The following day, as Simon and Rachel were finishing their morning meal together, there came a forced and hurried knock on the door.

"Simon! Rachel! Are you there? Let me enter. I bring important news!"

Rachel immediately recognized the excited voice and quickly rose to open the door. It was her younger brother, Benjamin, and he was totally devoid of breath.

"Benjamin!" cried a startled Rachel. "What has happened?"

"I hastened to arrive here before Simon's morning departure," he gasped as he stumbled into the house. "Father said that you two would surely want to know."

Simon stood and motioned for Benjamin to take his chair. "Calm yourself, Benjamin. Catch your breath, and then tell us of your news."

Benjamin paused for a moment, but could no longer stand to delay his announcement. "Simon,

Rachel," he said, anxiously looking up at them, "the great Matthias of Bethlehem has died!"

The two could do little more than stare at each other, but after a long moment of silence, Simon finally looked back at his brother-in-law. "Benjamin, are you certain? The great merchant, Matthias?"

Benjamin nodded his head. "Yes! A messenger arrived from Judea late last night to make the announcement to the city leaders."

Simon stared blankly at the wall before him in disbelief. He did not know Matthias personally, nor had he ever been privileged to meet him, but to Simon, and many others, Matthias was considered amongst the greatest of heroes. He was, without question, the most successful merchant in all of Judea, and was the kindest of men. He had been born in Damascus of Syria, but had lived much of his life in Bethlehem.

"But that is not all," said Benjamin, his words shook Simon from his mental stupor. "The messenger has requested that all men in the city who exceed the age of twenty meet with him in the synagogue tonight at the setting of the sun."

"But why would such a meeting be necessary?" asked Rachel, looking at her husband.

Simon appeared dismayed and shrugged his shoulders. "I do not know."

Benjamin had sufficiently regained his breath and was now up, pacing about the table. "It is being rumored that the messenger from Bethlehem wishes to discuss the dispensing of Matthias' wealth!"

"Then why would he be here?" questioned Rachel, shaking her head. "His wealth should be given to his family."

"Will you go to the meeting?" interrupted Benjamin, staring excitedly at Simon.

Simon looked at Rachel and after a long pause, said, "I suppose that I had better attend."

"I shall have your evening meal prepared early,"

11

said Rachel, nodding her head in agreement.

Simon attempted to perform his daily labors, but he could not take his mind off of Matthias and the meeting that was to take place later on that night. Simon had idolized Matthias for many years and had yearned with all his heart that he would one day become like the great merchant from Bethlehem.

The day passed ever so slowly, and the sun appeared to stand still in the sky. Simon thought that it would never reach the western hills, but after what seemed an eternity, the sun finally set over the horizon and with it, the men of Cyrene began to gather in the synagogue.

Simon, being one of the youngest to attend, took his place towards the back of the synagogue along with the other men of lesser age. The more prominent men of the city sat towards the front, while the Rabbi and Priests occupied the stand with a man whom Simon did not recognize, but whom he correctly identified as the messenger from Bethlehem.

When all appeared to be in order, the Rabbi stood to address the attentive congregation. "My dear brethren," he began, "as most of you are aware, it is with great sadness that we announce the passing of our most noble citizen and brother, Matthias of Bethlehem."

The crowd, having heard the news in advance, was not surprised, but each nodded their heads as a means of signaling their agreement with the Rabbi's description of this honorable man.

"Of course," continued the Rabbi, "we have not gathered here solely for the purpose of making this grave announcement." The Rabbi then turned to his right and gestured towards the messenger who sat behind him. "Nathaniel, of Bethlehem, has traveled a great distance on an errand from Demetrius, head servant of Matthias these many years, so that he might share with us news concerning the passing of our dear brother. Not even I know of the message which he shall share with us this night." The Rabbi nodded towards the messenger. "Brother Nathaniel, please come forward."

Nathaniel stood, and as he did so, a quiet hush fell over the congregation. Simon, being seated towards the back of the synagogue, strained to hear the man from Judea speak.

Nathaniel cleared his throat, paused for a long moment, and then began, "Brethren, I have traveled many days from Bethlehem to tell you of the passing of my master, Matthias. I come by way of commandment from Demetrius, he who has served Matthias faithfully for many years as his most trusted steward.

"As all of you are surely aware, Matthias attained much success as a merchant, and during his blessed lifetime he acquired a tremendous amount of wealth, most of which has already been graciously given to the poor who reside in Judea. But there yet remains a vast amount of riches, the balance of which Matthias desired to give unto his people, including those who reside here in the city of Cyrene."

Suddenly, there arose a great commotion amongst those in the congregation. Matthias' benevolence pleased them, especially since they would now be the beneficiaries of such kindness.

The messenger raised his hand to quiet the excited crowd. "My master, Matthias, was greatly troubled during the last fortnight of his life as he and Demetrius arduously attempted to discover a manner in which his wealth might properly be distributed to the people of Judea. He had almost given up hope and resigned himself to sure failure, when but three days prior to his death, he felt the God of Heaven inspire his mind as to what must be done."

One of the men from the city impatiently stood and cried out, "Please, Nathaniel, let there be no further delay. Tell us of this plan!"

13

"Yes, yes, on with it Nathaniel!" said another with equal agitation.

Nathaniel nodded. "Let it be so, and so I shall tell you." He paused momentarily to catch their full attention and then continued, "In the southern most part of Bethlehem, not far from master Matthias' estate, is a large cave, the location of which is well known. The cave has been filled with the remainder of his wealth, and to this day lies under heavy guard. No one, save Demetrius, is permitted to enter therein.

"At the end of the coming month, in celebration of the sacred Passover, there shall be organized a great race, which shall originate at the city of Damascus in Syria, and then conclude at the cave in Bethlehem. The race shall commence on the Tuesday preceding the Passover at the rising of the sun."

The men could no longer hold their exhilaration. "What of the money?!" They shouted. "Who is to get the money?!"

Nathaniel ignored their persistent inquiries and continued, "Matthias and Demetrius calculated that there is sufficient wealth in the cave to make a thousand men financially secure for the remainder of their lives."

The news brought an audible gasp from the crowd!

"Therefore," said Nathaniel, "the first thousand men to arrive at the cave shall share equally in the wealth that yet remains."

One of the leading Elders in the congregation stood and Nathaniel motioned for him to speak. "Brother Nathaniel, this is indeed a most benign act displayed by our dear brother, Matthias, but let us not forget that Damascus lies nearly a thousand miles from Cyrene. The labor alone of such a demanding journey would render any man exhausted. And yet, the conclusion of this sojourn would find us merely at the starting point of the race. We shall then be forced to retrace our steps southward an additional three or four

14

days of travel before we reach Bethlehem. Such would surely be an impossible task for anyone. It is most obvious that those who live in or about Judea shall enjoy a significant advantage over those of us who dwell here in Cyrene."

The crowd immediately began to murmur, for amidst their excitement, they had failed to recognize such an apparent obstacle.

"You are correct, my brother," replied Nathaniel. "I do not pretend to speak lightly of, or lessen the burden you shall face. It is most unfortunate that you reside such a great distance from our people in Judea. Matthias wished to make the task equal to all, but such was an impossibility. And with the knowledge that the majority of our people live in Judea, it seemed only just and right that such an event be held there. Damascus has been chosen as the starting point of the race, for it is the birthplace of Matthias. Bethlehem was chosen, obviously, because it is the city of his mortal departure."

The Elder thought for a moment, shrugged his shoulders and sat down, apparently content or at least pacified with Nathaniel's answer.

"Perhaps," said another man who now stood before the congregation, "those who wish to join this adventure will be better served if they will but sojourn by ship to the western shore of Phoenicia, and then ride by horse the remaining distance to the city of Damascus."

"Such a route is certainly a possibility," offered Nathaniel, "yet I chose not to speak of it, for there are many here this night who do not possess the means of purchasing a passage from Cyrene to the Phoenician coast."

Once again, the crowd began to stir uncomfortably as they slowly came to the realization that sharing in the great merchant's wealth would be no easy task. And, for many of them, the possibility of even partici-

15

pating in the race, seemed all but remote.

Nathaniel gazed out over the rumbling congregation, raised his brow and sighed, suddenly worn and tired from his tasking journey. "My dear brethren," he said as he lifted his hands once again to quiet the crowd. "I have come here this night to fulfill the errand entrusted to me by Demetrius. I have now done so. Please excuse my directness, for I do not wish to offend, but it is not my duty, nor is it my responsibility to assist you in your sojourn to Damascus.

"I shall repeat the message of my errand: on the Tuesday preceding the Passover at the rising of the sun, there shall commence a great race from the city of Damascus. At that time you shall be given a special mark, officially noting your entrance, and as proof that you have started in a legal manner with the others.

"Your objective is to arrive at the cave in the city of David as quickly as possible, for only the first thousand men shall be rewarded. It is not our concern by what manner you choose to travel or which route you take. Demetrius shall remain at the cave until all the wealth has been distributed, and if by fate you are blessed to arrive amongst the first thousand riders, then your efforts shall be rewarded with a substantial amount of wealth.

"If, however, your advent at the cave follows thereafter, then you shall depart with nothing to show for your hardship and toil. I am sorry, my esteemed brethren, but it is that simple. I bid you good fortune and God's blessings." Nathaniel then turned, respectfully nodded to the local leaders, and with equal abruptness exited the synagogue. He was never seen in the city again.

Amidst all the commotion of the night, young Simon had sat so very still and quiet, but inwardly his heart was racing. He had heard very little after the announcement that the first thousand men to reach the cave would be rewarded with enough wealth to last a lifetime!

After the meeting had been concluded and the congregation dismissed, Simon rushed home to share the exciting news with his beloved Rachel. As he walked through the darkened city, Simon could not help but envision what such a grand portion of Matthias' wealth would mean to him and his young family.

Chapter Four

Rachel stared at her husband in disbelief. "But Simon, Damascus is such a great distance from here," she said, "and it is sure to be a journey fraught with much danger and mishap."

Simon could see that he had indeed made a grave error. His boldness and abruptness in explaining the race had brought nothing but fright and concern to his young wife, something he had not anticipated, but should have expected.

He had thought only of the riches and the security they would bring. Never had he considered the situation through her eyes. He cautiously rose from his chair and walked over to Rachel, who sat on an old, wooden couch near the fire, and knelt before her.

"I realize that Damascus is indeed a great distance from Cyrene, Rachel," he said quietly, gently taking her hand in his, "but there will be many who race, so I doubt that I shall ever be entirely alone."

Rachel looked up at her husband, the flickering light from the flames revealed tears in her eyes. "Simon, I fear for your life," she whispered. "I do not wish you to go. Surely you can understand how I feel."

"But Rachel," he pleaded, "think of the riches that are to be gained. Nathaniel said that there would be sufficient wealth to last us the rest of our lives. It could be the answer to our prayers."

Rachel suddenly stood and displayed a rage which Simon had never seen from her before. "I do not care about the wealth! I care for you!"

"But I can do it!" he implored as he stood to face her. "I know that I can be amongst the first thousand riders to arrive at the cave."

By now Rachel was sobbing. "Did you not hear me?" she cried. "I do not want the money if it means the possibility of losing you." She did not wish to hurt him, but fear had rendered her unsparing and her words were spoken with no prior thought. "And besides, what chance have you? The only animal we possess is that old mule outside. It would die before it ever made it half the distance to Damascus. And we have not sufficient money to buy a passage across the Great Sea." Rachel paused, trying to calm herself. "Simon, you have not the means to arrive at the start of the race, let alone finish it."

Rachel dropped her head and continued to cry. Simon said nothing. There were only the sounds of Rachel's quiet sobs. Her words, though, had cut him deeply. Perhaps because he knew that they were true. Not since before suffering his terrible accident had he felt such an enthralling passion for something as he did about the race and the grand possibilities it presented.

But as he stood there before his sobbing wife in that small, darkened house, he knew that his hopes and dreams had been destroyed. Rachel was correct; he did not have enough money for passage on a ship, nor did he possess an animal which could carry him on such a demanding journey.

He dejectedly nodded. "You speak the truth, Rachel," he said in surrender. "I have not a chance." He then turned and walked slowly into the other room. His shoulders, which had stood proud and full of hope when he entered the house that evening, once again hung disheartened and defeated before him.

Simon slept fitfully that night, but Rachel lay wide awake in the lonely darkness. She was relieved that Simon would not be attempting the race, but to her, it was a hollow victory. She took no joy in seeing his renewed passion being devastated in such a manner. Perhaps it was selfish of her, but she simply loved Simon too deeply to see him place his life in such perilous danger. It will take time, she thought, as she covered her sleeping husband with a light blanket, but Simon would soon forget all about the race. She was certain of it.

It was several days later, after Simon had arrived home from his daily labors in the field, that there was once again a knock at the door. Simon was occupied washing the day's dust from his face and hands, so it was Rachel who responded to the visitor.

"Father!" she said, opening the door. "What a pleasant surprise. Please, come in."

The old man smiled and nodded as he entered the humble dwelling. "Good evening, Rachel."

She motioned to a chair at the table, "Would you like to sit down?" There was no reason to feel un-comfortable, yet Rachel sensed a deep foreboding. "Is everything alright, father?"

The old man seemed somewhat preoccupied and nervous. He was looking about the house when her question caught him by surprise. "Uh...yes, yes. All is well." There was a short pause. "I have come to speak with Simon. Is he here?"

Rachel carefully observed her father. Why would he

20

be asking for Simon? The two men had never become close, and in truth, Rachel's father was at times critical of Simon's inability to provide for his only daughter. "He is in the back washing for the evening meal," she said. "I shall tell him that you are here."

Once again the old man nodded. "Thank you, Rachel."

It was not long until Simon entered the house with Rachel following closely behind him. "I bid you a pleasant evening, Jacob," said a surprised Simon. "Will you stay and sup with us?"

"No thank you, Simon. Your invitation is indeed most kind, but I wish only to discuss a matter of business with you."

Simon sat in a chair opposite his father-in-law. "Business? What kind of business?"

Jacob hesitated and looked up at Rachel who now stood behind her husband. He then turned his gaze back towards Simon. "It is regarding Matthias and the race." He instinctively raised his eyes to once again look at his daughter. It did not surprise him that a sudden expression of shock and panic appeared in her face, but she said nothing.

Jacob's answer caused Simon to stir in his chair. "What about the race?"

Jacob had planned on showing extreme restraint, but now decided to abandon his strategy of caution. "I would like for the two of us to form an alliance."

"An alliance?" questioned Simon.

"Yes," said Jacob, leaning forward. "You see, I had contemplated entering the race myself, but I am now too far advanced in years to endure such a journey, and my sons are not yet old enough to qualify by age." Jacob paused and stared directly at his son-in-law. "But you Simon," he continued, "you could make such a journey."

Rachel was about to interrupt the two men, but to her surprise, and considerable joy, Simon bridled his emotions. He had previously made the mistake of becoming overly excited about the race, and thus had set himself up for a terrible emotional fall.

"It is impossible, Jacob," he said, shaking his head. "I have not an animal to ride nor can I afford the passage to Phoenicia."

"This I realize, Simon," replied Jacob with a pleading voice. "It is for that reason that I have requested that we form a partnership."

Simon again shook his head. "I am afraid that I do not understand, Jacob."

"I shall pay for the passage," said Jacob, pointing to himself, "and give unto you sufficient funds to purchase a sound horse upon your arrival at the Phoenician coast."

Rachel had stood quietly listening to the two men, but she could no longer restrain herself. "But father," she argued, "your circumstances are almost as meager as ours. You cannot afford to spend such money any more than we can."

Jacob calmly looked at his daughter. "That is not true, Rachel. I have managed to save a little money. It is not much, but enough to purchase the passage and a good horse."

"But father," she cried, raising her hands into the air, "it is all you possess. Are you willing to risk it all on a mere chance such as this?"

Simon's enthusiasm had returned and he did not permit Jacob to answer his daughter. "A partnership, Jacob? Tell me exactly what you are thinking."

The two men drew closer together. "Very well, this is what I propose. As stated, I shall pay for the passage and the horse. You, of course, will ride in the race. Upon your return to Cyrene, we shall then equally divide the wealth you receive when you arrive at the cave."

Rachel interrupted, "And what if he arrives after Matthias' wealth has been disbursed? What shall happen then?"

Jacob bowed his head, not wanting to acknowledge such a possibility. "Then," he said softly, "we gain nothing. I shall lose my humble savings and Simon will lose the investment of time." Jacob carefully lifted his head and stared at Simon. Their eyes met. "But," he continued, "I think that we are both more than willing to take such a risk."

Simon returned Jacob's gaze and ever so slightly nodded his agreement. That was all Jacob needed to see. He shook Simon's hand and then rose from his chair and politely excused himself, not daring to look at his daughter.

On his way out the door he paused and turned to Simon. "You will need to depart Cyrene at least a week in advance of the race. That should allow you ample time to reach Damascus." With that, Jacob turned and walked out into the night, shutting the door behind him.

Neither Simon or Rachel spoke. There was a deafening silence that was interrupted only by the occasional sounds of the crackling fire. After a long moment, Rachel opened her mouth to speak, but Simon calmly interrupted her.

"Rachel, please, permit me to speak first."

There was a short pause, after which Rachel relaxed her body and gently nodded her agreement.

"Rachel, I cherish you and Rebecca more than you could ever dream possible. I would never do anything to hurt you or cause you harm, but this is something that I must do." Simon uncomfortably began to pace about the small room, choosing his words with great caution. "It is my responsibility to care for you and Rebecca, but unfortunately, I have failed miserably in my calling as your provider."

Rachel warmly stepped towards him. "That is not true, Simon. Rebecca and I both love you very much."

Simon turned to his young wife. "I know you

23

do Rachel, but by the grace of heaven I have been granted this one opportunity, which will most likely never present itself again. I cannot let it pass if I am to ever live with myself. If I fail, then let it be so, but at least I will have made the attempt."

Rachel looked at her husband and admiringly gazed into his eyes. Therein, once again, she beheld deep emotion and hope burning brightly within his soul, just as it had upon his return from the meeting with Nathaniel a few nights ago.

She did not wish to admit it, but she was proud of Simon, proud of the fact that he would do this for her, and perhaps, she thought, this could be what Simon needed to restore his lost confidence and passion for life. Rachel stepped towards Simon and embraced him with all the love she could summon from her aching heart. "I know that you must go, Simon," she whispered. "I only ask one thing of you."

He gently withdrew to gaze upon her beautiful face. There he beheld an expression of deep concern. "Anything," he said.

She raised her hand to brush the hair that fell over his eyes. "Then please, do not ever put your life in danger. It would never be worth the risk."

Simon tenderly wrapped his arms around Rachel and held her close. He could feel her body tremble as she tried not to cry, but she could do little to stem the flood of tears that flowed from her eyes. "You must not worry, Rachel. I promise that I will come home safely to you. The God of Heaven shall guide my path."

Chapter Five

Simon stood on the ship's deck at night, gazing up at the stars in the still, black sky. The Great Sea was calm. There was a gentle but steady breeze, the sailing was smooth. He had boarded the massive Phoenician freighter two days earlier at the port in Cyrene, and thence the ship was scheduled to stop at the island of Cyprus, where weary passengers would disembark and others would board the ship for the brief journey to the coastal city of Sidon in Phoenicia.

Bidding farewell to Rachel and Rebecca had been more difficult than Simon had expected. Rachel, however, had been courageous, limiting herself to a few tears and enthusiastically wishing her husband much success and God's blessings. She obviously still feared for Simon's safety, but she made a noble attempt to disguise her feelings and hide the wary emotions she felt in her heart.

As he stared at the blanket of stars in the darkened

sky, Simon suddenly found himself in the midst of prayer, an act not foreign to him since his mother had taught him to pray while he was yet a small lad. "Please, dear God of Heaven," he whispered out loud, "guide my path and go before me, that my journey may be swift and fruitful." He paused, fearful that perhaps his plea had not been specific enough, and so as not to be misunderstood by Deity, he continued, "Help me, that I shall not depart from the cave unrewarded." He then turned from the open sea and descended below the deck where he slept soundly for the remainder of the night.

The Phoenician freighter arrived at Cyprus the following evening at the setting of the sun. As it entered the island's small port, Simon veiled his face with the hooded coat and climbed onto the deck to enjoy the fresh sea air and the sight of land for the first time in three days. Many of the passengers disembarked the ship, but relatively few people boarded for the brief trip to the mainland.

Simon, however, did notice four men board the vessel as it was about to depart for the Phoenician coast. The man who walked in front of the other three, and who appeared to be their leader, was tall, perhaps over six feet. His shoulders were broad and strong, and his hair was a light brown color, as was his beard. But it was not his large stature, nor his physical appearance which at first drew Simon's attention, rather it was what Simon beheld in this good man's eyes; for never before had Simon witnessed such kindness and peace.

After boarding the freighter, the four men gathered their humble belongings and went below to rest from their labors. The evening air soon turned cold as the sun completely descended below the horizon, but Simon remained on deck, enjoying his solitude in the darkness of the night. An hour or so thereafter, he heard footsteps from behind him growing louder, and he turned to see the stranger who had boarded the freighter at Cyprus approaching.

Simon quickly cloaked his face with the hood and nodded to the stranger.

"A pleasant evening to you," said the man.

"And to you also," replied Simon. "It is a cold night. I expected no one else to be above deck."

The stranger rubbed his arms to warm them. "I was somewhat restless and thought to seek solitude amidst the cool air." There was a brief pause. "And to where do you journey, young friend?"

"My final destination is Bethlehem," replied Simon, "but I must first travel to Damascus."

The man nodded. "You must be one of the many who race for Matthias' wealth?"

Simon appeared surprised. "Yes . . . yes I am."

The stranger looked out over the calm sea which shimmered from the light of the moon, saying, "It is indeed a most splendid night."

Simon rested his arms on the ship's railing and breathed in the smell of the sea. "It is indeed."

It was then, without prior warning, that the man turned his gaze towards Simon and said, "You must understand, Simon, that it is of little import."

Puzzled, Simon replied, "I am sorry?"

The stranger placed his left hand on Simon's shoulder and then slowly lifted his other hand to Simon's face and carefully removed the protecting hood. Had it been anyone else, Simon would have quickly withdrawn, but for some reason, unknown even to him, he willingly accepted this intrusion of his privacy. "Your face," said the man, with a compassion that Simon had never felt before. "The appearance of your face is not important."

Simon remained silent, slightly bowing his head.

"You have much to offer the world, Simon, and it is a terrible waste for you to hide your wonderful talents and gifts behind this hood."

Simon was about to explain the many reasons for hiding from the world the way he did and how his deformed face made him feel, but as he gazed up into the man's face, his speech deserted him. Simon's eyes began to fill with tears and his lips quivered as years of frustration escaped his aching heart.

The stranger then tenderly grasped Simon by the shoulders and pulled him close. "Be calm, young Simon. All shall be well. You will see. In time, peace will come to your soul and you will rise above your challenges. This I know."

"Forgive me, sir," said Simon apologetically, "for I do not wish to offend, but what would you know of my pains and sorrows?"

The stranger faintly smiled at Simon's question, but then after looking towards the heavens in pensive thought, a serious countenance appeared in his face. Turning back towards Simon, he said, "Believe me, Simon, I know well of what I speak."

Meeting the man's powerful gaze, it was as if the stranger could see into Simon's soul, and it was then that Simon knew that the man who stood before him spoke the truth. Simon did not understand how, but in some manner, inexplicable and yet so very real, the stranger truly did understand the pain in his heart.

"It will take time, my young friend, but think of what I have said."

Simon quieted his sobs and nodded his understanding, surprised and overcome by the tranquil influence he felt emanating from the stranger. "I will," he said. "And thank you."

The man smiled, patting Simon on the back. "It is well, Simon. I bid you a most pleasant evening." The man then turned and descended below the deck. Simon, his mind bewildered and somewhat troubled by the power of the stranger, followed shortly thereafter.

Later that night, as Simon lay in his bed, he could do little more than think of the kind man. There was indeed something so very different about him, for he truly possessed a virtue, a goodness and a love that Simon had never felt before in another human being.

As he fell into a fitful sleep, Simon suddenly remembered that the stranger had called him by name. But how could he have done so when Simon had never revealed it to him? Simon shook his head; he must have been mistaken.

It was during the third watch, in the early hours of the morning, that the raging tempest struck with awful fury. The crests of the powerful waves topped the ship's gigantic masts and came crashing down onto the massive freighter. Simon was awakened in his bunk by the volatile movements of the vessel, whereupon he hastened up the stairs which lead to the deck. Simon could barely manage to retain his balance, for it was raining heavily and the wind was blowing with horrifying force. The captain of the ship desperately yelled instructions to his men, but his attempts were futile, for he could not be heard above the raging sea.

Amidst the ensuing turmoil, Simon noticed that one of the men traveling with the stranger had ascended from below and appeared to be inspecting the severity of the storm. His countenance revealed concern, yet he was not frightened as the others, such as Simon, who was by then filled with a dreadful panic.

After observing the storm for but a brief time, the man hastily retreated below the deck, and it was only a moment later that the kind stranger appeared. He also gazed at the ferocious storm, but to Simon's surprise, he remained calm. Amidst the awful tempest, he majestically stood and walked to the ship's bow. Once there, he lifted his right hand over the great tumultuous sea, and in a soft voice that pierced the frightful darkness, he commanded, saying, "Peace, be still."

The raging elements immediately obeyed the supreme command, as the storm miraculously abated, leaving the sea, once again, still and peaceful. The stranger, being followed by curious and bewildered eyes, returned to his humble room below the deck.

Simon was more than mesmerized by the miracle! Who is this man, he thought, who even possesses the power to command the mighty winds and the waves? Surely, he is more than just a man!

No one on the ship, including Simon, slept for the remainder of the night, excepting he who had quieted the storm and the three passengers who sojourned with him. All others were in dismay after observing the great miracle and everyone visited amongst themselves, attempting to discover the true identity of their benefactor. But there was no one who had previously seen or heard of him, save a few passengers who had heard rumors of a similar incident several months earlier on the Sea of Galilee.

The following morning, shortly before their arrival in Phoenicia, Simon timidly approached the small group of men as they visited on deck. He desperately wanted to speak to them, but stopped short of his desire when he drew nigh enough to hear their conversation.

"Master, where are we to go from Sidon in Phoenicia?" asked one of the men.

"My beloved John," the man replied. "We shall be joined by the others in Sidon, and thence we shall journey to Jerusalem to celebrate the Passover."

One of the men suddenly appeared worried and stepped forward. "Do you think that is wise, Master? You are surely aware of the terrible feelings of malice which there await you."

"Yes, Master," said John with equal concern. "Let us not go down to Jerusalem, for truly your life is valued but little amongst the leaders there. Perhaps we shall be better served if we instead journey to Galilee where trusted friends await."

Their Master looked tenderly upon the three young

men who accompanied him and sighed deeply. "No, my dear friends. It must needs be that I go to Jerusalem. For shall I not drink of the cup which my Father has given me? It is for this purpose that I came into the world; to do the will of Him that sent me. Fear not, all shall be well."

Simon did not fully comprehend the words he had just heard, but of this much he was sure; the life of this good man was in certain and perilous danger if he was to ever enter Jerusalem again.

Simon felt a great yearning to follow after this small band of men as they disembarked the freighter, but he suddenly remembered his errand. He reluctantly left the port and entered the city of Sidon, searching for a good horse. Then on he would travel to Damascus and the great race.

But as he walked, he could do little to erase from his mind the image of a man who could not only calm a raging sea, but a person's troubled heart as well. How he hoped that their paths would one day cross again.

Chapter Six

Simon eyed the white stallion with great excitement. It was indeed a magnificent beast. One, he thought, worthy and capable of enduring the hardships of the race.

"How much are you asking?" inquired Simon, speaking to the stableman, but continuing to inspect the horse.

"Fifty pence," said the man. "And do not offend me by haggling over the price. Word of the race has spread to every nation in the civilized world and there is much competition for such animals."

The price of the horse was indeed extremely inflated, but the stableman had little need to exaggerate its true worth. He was right; if Simon chose not to purchase the horse for the asking price, then with certainty another rider would gladly pay the requested amount.

"But," pleaded Simon, "I have only fifty pence total,

which was to be used for the purchase of a horse and food for the race. I beg of you, kind sir, to reduce your price that I may retain at least ten pence for myself."

The man laughed heartily. "You have much humor, young man," he said as he slapped Simon on the back. But after quieting his boisterous laugh and carefully observing the dejected expression on Simon's cloaked face, he could easily discern that Simon's plea had indeed been sincere. He then paused and thoughtfully grabbed his bearded chin. "I will tell you what I shall do. Let it not be said that I have left a man desolate in his time of need. I will sell the horse to you for forty-five pence, thus allowing you a full five pence for the race." The man then lifted his hand and shook his finger at Simon, saying, "But let the haggling cease now or I shall lose my sense of mercy and sell the stallion to another."

Simon looked at his money and despondently sighed. He was fully aware that five pence would not last him through the race, but he had very little choice in the matter. He desperately needed a horse and could not concern himself with the problems of the morrow. He reached out to grasp the man's hand. "So be it. Forty-five pence for the horse . . . if you provide for me a saddle as well."

The man hesitated and was about to argue Simon's newly stated condition, but thought better of it. After all, what was an old, worn saddle to him? "It is well, my young haggler," he said, shaking Simon's hand. "We have a deal."

The race would not commence for another four days, and since the distance to Damascus was but sixty miles, Simon thought it best to complete the journey in two days, thus allowing both he and the stallion a day of rest prior to the race.

Simon saddled the stallion and loaded his simple provisions, which included water, a small amount of food and a bed-roll, and headed directly east into the morning sun. He carefully placed his hand into his bag to make certain that he carried the map which Jacob had given to him prior to boarding the Phoenician freighter in Cyrene.

The map had been prepared by Rachel's uncle, a man well traveled in and about Galilee and Judea. The three men had sat together in Jacob's house the night before Simon's departure from Cyrene planning the route which Simon should take.

It was decided that he would leave Damascus, traveling in a southwesterly direction on the great Syrian highway until he arrived at the town of Capernaum on the northwestern shore of the Sea of Galilee. Thence, he would continue directly along the sea's western shore, leading him to the famed River Jordan which he would follow through the rich Jordan Valley to the ancient city of Jericho. From there, he would make the brief journey west to Jerusalem, before traveling south, the final six miles to Bethlehem and, of course, the cave containing Matthias' vast wealth.

There was the possibility of a shorter route, but Rachel's uncle feared it to be less traveled and held a greater chance for trouble and mishap. The total distance of the race was but 180 miles, as best as could be calculated, and Simon hoped to complete the journey in three days. The race was to commence on the Tuesday preceding the Passover, thus Simon planned on arriving at the cave sometime late Thursday evening.

He considered attempting the journey in a shorter period of time, but such a strategy could only invite disaster. An animal could only be expected to endure so much under such demanding conditions. It would be useless to travel a more exacting pace, for the horse would simply die of exhaustion, leaving no hope at all of ever finishing the race.

Simon also contemplated traveling during the night,

in addition to his daytime riding, in an attempt to gain ground on the other riders who would surely cease their travels at the setting of the sun. But once again, Simon figured that riding in the blackness of the night would put the horse in jeopardy of suffering an injury.

His only hope of success was to sojourn during the light of day at a steady enough pace which would take him to the cave amongst the first thousand riders, but which his horse could also endure.

The two day journey to Damascus was uneventful. Simon was forced, however, to transverse the steep mountains of the Lebanon range which lie between Sidon and Damascus, but he completed the first day's thirty miles just as the sun was setting over the colorful horizon.

He camped a short distance off of the road and rose early the following morning with the new light of day. He easily made the second thirty miles, arriving in Damascus while the sun was yet a good distance from the western hills.

Simon, however, was aghast at the scene which greeted him as he approached the outskirts of the city! He had figured the race to be popular, but never did he consider that the response would be so great. An endless number of camps had been established outside of the city's walls and men from every known nation and culture were everywhere to be seen.

Their response to Simon's arrival was mixed. Some of the other riders nodded and gestured a kind welcome as he rode by, but the majority of them warily stared back at him as if he were a vulture, competing for their prey.

Regardless of their welcome or contempt, Simon's heart sank when he saw the never ending sea of riders, figuring that his chances of arriving at the cave with the first thousand men had dramatically and bleakly diminished.

It was not long, however, that Simon located an

unoccupied camp near the city's northern wall. It was there that he dismounted the horse, unpacked his provisions and built a small fire in order to prepare his evening meal. There he would remain, cautiously watching over the stallion until the commencement of the race.

It was early Tuesday, hours before sunrise, that the large camp came to life. The riders were finishing their morning meal and packing their animals before making their way to the starting position along the great highway which leads from Damascus to Galilee. Some rode horses, while others settled on camels or mules.

Because of the vast numbers which had entered the race, the starting line had been officially extended for miles, affording as many riders as possible the opportunity of gathering near the line itself, thus assuring a fair start for all.

Simon donned his hooded cloak and made his way to an open spot on the line and there dismounted his horse, permitting it to rest until the start of the race.

"Greetings to you, young man," came a voice from Simon's right. He turned and beheld an older man extending his hand.

Observing kindness in the old man's eyes, Simon grasped his hand, saying, "And a pleasant morning to you also."

"I am Matthew, and come from Judea."

Simon nodded. "I am most pleased to meet you, Matthew. I am Simon, from Cyrene."

Matthew lifted his eyes. "Cyrene?! Such a great distance you have traveled, young friend."

Simon shook his head. "The journey was not so long. I traveled from Cyrene to the Phoenician coast by ship. The remainder of the journey took but two days."

It was then that the two men were interrupted by an angry voice from behind them. "It matters little of the route which brought you here, for your journey shall profit you but nothing!"

They turned to see the Roman soldier dismounting his horse; his eyes revealed his arrogance and his loathing for the two men. "You should never have made the attempt!"

"All have an equal chance," said Simon rather timidly, not quite secure in his response.

"What chance have you?" scoffed the Roman. "Surely you cannot hope to arrive at the cave before the many trained soldiers and riders who have entered the race?"

Simon only lowered his head. He turned to Matthew who stood at his side. "I thought that the race was meant solely for the people of Judah?"

The older man sighed. "It was so at the beginning, my friend, but word of the race soon reached Pontius Pilate, procurator of Jerusalem, and he ordered the race open to any and all who wished to enter, knowing full well that much of the wealth would be gained by the better equipped and trained soldiers who serve him. At first, Demetrius refused this outlandish condition, but later agreed to Pilate's demand when the ruler threatened to storm the cave and seize the wealth therein."

"You may as well give up now," said the Roman, indignantly staring at the two men. "There is little to be gained here for such as you."

Simon was somewhat intimidated, but Matthew did not waver. "We have come this far, my good man. Surely there is no harm in carrying on a few more days."

"It is just as well," said the soldier, mounting his horse. "We shall have need of riders to shield our backs from thieves as we travel." He then scornfully spat on the ground before the two men and recklessly rode off further down the highway.

Matthew placed his hand on Simon's trembling

shoulder in a calming gesture. "Do not allow such a one as he to worry you, young Simon. But let us ride and pray that the God of Heaven guides our path."

Simon's face brightened and he nodded. "It shall be so." There was a short pause. "Did you say that you come from Judea, Matthew?"

"You heard correctly, my young friend. Specifically, Bethlehem."

"Bethlehem? Then you are but riding to the town where you presently reside."

"That is true."

Simon was suddenly struck with an idea. He removed the map of his route from the small bag and shared it with the older man while inquiring of its accuracy.

"If I were to travel to Bethlehem in the manner which you have chosen, then this is precisely the route which I would take," said the older man, pointing to the map.

Simon was pleased, but after further considering Matthew's words he asked, "Are you not to travel in a similar manner?"

The man thought deeply, not sure if he wanted to share his plans, but then saw no harm in it. "No, Simon," he whispered, making certain that his words could not be heard by other riders. "I shall ride to the Sea of Galilee where I have hidden a small boat. This I will take to the southern shore where my wife awaits with a fresh horse. I figure to gain a few precious hours by utilizing this strategy."

Simon smiled at Matthew. "Your route is indeed well planned. I wish you every success. I pray that we both make the cave while there yet remains wealth to share."

The older man affectionately patted Simon on the back. "Such is my prayer as well."

The two friends mounted their horses and looked towards the eastern horizon. Shades of red began to fill the dimly lit sky. Servants of Demetrius made haste as they passed amongst the many riders, placing a special mark on the back of their right hand, so as to indicate their official and legal start in the race.

There was soon a great quiet amongst the anxious participants. By this time they had strewn out along the highway for miles. All was in readiness; there was little else to do but wait for the rising of the sun. Within minutes, a sliver of red rose above the eastern hills, whereupon the great multitude of riders, literally thousands of them, burst forward, shouting their exhilaration as they went! Simon, his heart pounding like a beating drum, rode towards the front!

Chapter Seven

Simon slowly awoke as the stranger gently shook him, saying, "Are you well, my son?"

Simon reluctantly opened his eyes and saw the stranger above him. Startled, he attempted to rise, but fell back to the earth. His head was pounding with excruciating pain.

"Be still, young man," commanded the stranger in a comforting voice. "All shall be well. Lay for awhile and rest yourself."

Simon closed his eyes and breathed deeply. He was barely conscious and lingered in a darkened stupor. For the moment, he had forgotten where he was and the circumstances which had brought him there. The stranger removed his outer garment and placed it under Simon's head. Turning to his daughter who stood beside him, he said, "Go with haste and bring some water for this good man that we may cleanse his wounds and give him to drink."

The young girl nodded and quickly ran to their well in accordance with her father's request. It was but a short time later that she returned with a small bucket filled with cold water and some bandages which her mother had prepared.

The man took the bucket and the bandages from his daughter. "Bless you, my dear one," he said, looking into her eyes. "Let us hope that we can help this man whom the God of Heaven has caused to come to us."

He dipped one of the bandages into the cool water and carefully began to cleanse the caked blood and dirt from Simon's forehead and face. After much of the blood had been wiped away, the stranger could see the awful looking gash just above Simon's left eye. He shook his head back and forth and sighed; there was no telling what injuries this young man had sustained.

The cool water seemed to revive Simon and again he slowly opened his eyes, but winced as his newly acquired consciousness awakened his sense of pain. As before, he saw the stranger kneeling over him. His vision at first was blurred, but it became clearer as he opened and closed his eyes several times.

"Who are you?" mumbled Simon, looking up at his unknown benefactor.

"I am Jairus, leader of the synagogue here in Capernaum. And this is my daughter, Leah."

Simon instinctively lifted his hand to touch his forehead from whence came his pain. As he did so, he could feel the torn flesh and the blood oozing from the wound. "What has happened to me?" he asked.

Jairus dipped the bandage into the cool water once again and continued to clean Simon's face. "I am not sure, young man. It is apparent that you were riding through our field last night and you must have fallen from your horse, or else it was frightened and threw you. In any case, you hit your head on the ground and sustained an injury, how serious I know not."

41

Simon's memory slowly returned. "Of course," he whispered. "The race. I was riding at the setting of the sun and lost my way." An expression of deep concern suddenly crossed his face. "The stallion! Where is my horse?!"

Jairus patted Simon on the shoulder as he continued to wipe cool water across his forehead. "Calm yourself, my friend. Your horse is being well cared for by my servant. Even as we speak, it rests in our stable feeding on a goodly supply of grain."

Simon relaxed, but with sudden urgency he remembered his errand and duty. "But I must continue to Jericho. I cannot delay a moment longer." Once again he started to rise, but just as before, he began to lose consciousness.

"I am sorry, young friend, but you are in no condition to continue your journey," said Jairus. "I beg of you to rest yourself. Abide with us but a few days and all shall be well."

"A few days?" Simon cried softly. "I cannot remain here even an hour. For if I do, then all the wealth in the cave shall be gone upon my arrival."

"Ah, yes," said Jairus. "You must be one of the many who race towards Bethlehem."

Simon paused. "You know of the race?"

Jairus looked surprised. "Does not everyone? I understand your earnestness . . . forgive me, friend, but what is your name?"

Simon breathed deeply, not believing his ill fortune. "Simon . . . my name is Simon . . . from Cyrene."

"Well, Simon of Cyrene, it is true that I know of the race, and I am also well aware of the small fortune you seek. But is wealth more valuable to you than your life?"

Simon only closed his eyes and sighed in despair. He said nothing.

Once the wound was cleaned and bandaged, Jairus thought it best to take Simon into his house where he could rest comfortably and be properly cared for. He gently knelt beside Simon and lifted his upper torso to a sitting position, causing Simon to groan in pain. Jairus then placed Simon's arm around his own shoulder and lifted him to his feet.

Together the two men slowly made their way from the field to the house. As they went, Jairus spoke to his daughter, "Go, my child, and inform your mother that we bring an injured man. Make sure that a bed is prepared for him."

"It shall be done, my father," she said, dutifully obeying.

Leah opened the door as her father and Simon arrived on the porch, where Jairus' wife was waiting for them as they entered. She had a look of grave concern on her face when she saw Simon.

"Where shall I put him?" asked Jairus, breathing deeply, exhausted from his efforts.

"Bring him into our room, Jairus. He shall be cooler there," she tenderly commanded, preceding her husband into the room.

Jairus placed Simon on the bed and lowered him slowly onto his back, resting his head on one of the pillows, while his wife lifted Simon's feet onto the other end of the bed and then covered him with a light blanket.

Miriam, Jairus' wife, then turned to her daughter who had been standing in the doorway and said, "Leah, please bring more water and fresh bandages."

"What may I do to assist, Miriam?" asked Jairus.

Miriam carefully removed the bloody bandage from Simon's head. "I shall need herbs for the wound, Jairus. Will you get them for me?"

"Most assuredly," he replied, leaving the room in haste.

A moment later, Leah returned, placing the bucket of water on the floor near her mother and the bandages on the bed. "Will he be alright, mother?" she asked, looking at Simon, who was by now attempting to open his eyes.

Miriam slowly and carefully cleansed the wound, at the same time she looked intently at Simon's eyes. "It is difficult to say, my daughter. The wound is fairly deep, but we shall apply herbs and a good dressing to it." She paused for a moment. "But I am more concerned about the wounds inside his head, if there be any. He appears to have lost his sight many years ago in his right eye during a terrible accident that also caused the scarring of his face, but his left eye is responding well to the light, so let us be hopeful that all shall be well with him."

It was then that Jairus entered the room carrying a tiny bowl which he placed on the small, wooden table near the bed. "Will this suffice, Miriam?"

"More than enough," she responded.

Once the wound had been thoroughly cleansed, Miriam carefully sprinkled into it a small amount of the healing herbs, then dressed it.

As she finished, Simon finally succeeded in opening his eyes. There at his side sat Miriam, while Jairus and Leah stood nearby.

"Where am I?" he hazily asked.

"Do not be concerned, young man," she calmly responded. "You are amongst friends. My husband tells me you had a bad fall."

Simon strained to think back to the preceding night, his memory was still vague. "Yes, I did . . . I think so . . . I must have." He looked towards the window. "What hour is it?"

"Early morning," responded Jairus. "The sun has barely risen."

Simon attempted to sit up. "Then all is not lost. I must continue the race." But his head immediately began to spin and throb as he raised himself up from the bed. His head then dropped back onto the pillow. Simon closed his eyes and fell into a deep sleep.

"He will rest for a few hours," said Miriam, rising from the bed. "Let us leave him in peace."

"Shall I go for a doctor?" asked Jairus as the three of them quietly left the room.

Miriam stopped for a moment and looked back at Simon. "I do not think so. He needs a few days of rest and some good food, and I believe he shall be fine."

Jairus nodded his approval. "I will see to his horse and then I have some work to do in the western field. I shall return at the noon hour. Call if you have need of me." He then turned to his daughter. "Leah, I think it best that you remain in the house today, should your mother have need of your assistance."

"Be not concerned," said Miriam. "All shall be well."

Chapter Eight

It was later that afternoon, as Jairus and his family sat finishing their midday meal, that Simon slowly walked into the room. Miriam and Jairus stood to assist him, but Simon calmed them and motioned for them to sit.

"Be at peace, my dear friends, I feel much better. My head hurts but very little, and the dizziness has completely left me."

Jairus arose and led Simon to a chair at the table. "The healing herbs have once again shown their great worth," said Jairus, looking admiringly at his wife.

She nodded her agreement. "We are most pleased for you, young friend," she said. "Surely, you must be hungry."

"I am," said Simon. "I ate but very little during the race yesterday, for I feared that it would delay my progress. But I can ill afford the loss of more time. Already the other riders have gained today's light.

Therefore, I must be off at once if I am to have any chance of arriving at the cave while the wealth remains."

But Miriam would not permit it. "I shall not allow you to leave, young Simon, until you have eaten something and restored your strength. For if you do not, then you shall never survive the race."

Simon paused and then nodded his acceptance. It was her home and here he would obey. Besides, he truly wanted for food. "It is well, my dear woman. I gratefully accept your offer."

Miriam grinned and then turned to Leah who stood at her side. "Daughter, please bring our guest food to eat and water to drink."

Leah responded without hesitation and soon was placing a bounty of food before Simon. "My sincerest thanks," said Simon, looking up at Leah.

Leah, being but fourteen years of age, blushed at Simon's innocent gaze and attention.

"Is she not wonderful?" asked Jairus.

"Indeed she is," replied Simon.

"We call her our miracle child," said Miriam.

Simon drank from the goblet and said, "Miracle child? Why do you call her such?" Simon assumed that perhaps the couple had experienced difficulty in conceiving their daughter. He certainly was not prepared for Jairus' answer.

"It is because she was once dead," Jairus explained, "and then was restored to life."

The goblet in Simon's hand dropped to the floor! "Dead?!" he questioned, his eyes filled with amazement. "What do you mean, dead?"

Jairus looked at Simon. "Just as I have stated; Leah died from a serious illness and was then restored to life."

Simon turned his gaze to Miriam as if questioning the truth of what Jairus had told him. She nodded her agreement with her husband's words. "He speaks the truth, Simon. Leah was dead and her life was then restored to her."

Simon looked at Jairus once again. "How did this happen? How did she return from amongst the dead?"

Jairus settled back into his chair. "It was two years ago," he began, "that Leah was suddenly stricken with a dreadful illness. We, of course, did all within our power to heal her of this affliction, but our efforts and those of the physicians were unsuccessful. We kept a constant vigil at her bedside both night and day with the hope that she would somehow survive, but we could see that life was ever so slowly leaving her. Leah's skin became pale, her breathing very shallow, and her eyes revealed but little light. We resigned ourselves to her sure fate and attempted to prepare for the loss of our only child. Our hearts were filled with the deepest of sorrow and despair as we were forced to sit and helplessly watch our sweet Leah pass from this world.

"It was then that I received word from my brother that the Messiah and His followers had arrived at the port here in Capernaum."

"The Messiah?" questioned Simon.

"Yes," said Jairus. "The Messiah. Although I must confess that at that time, I was not sure of my belief. For you see, I had heard of the coming of a great Prophet and His mighty works, but I had never before seen Him personally. Whether He was a fraud or a true Man of God, I knew not, but of all that I had heard of Him, I could not question His great power. So when I learned of His arrival at Capernaum, I immediately went to beseech His help."

"And you met this . . . this Messiah?" asked Simon, his excitement growing with each passing minute.

"Yes, and when I finally reached Him," continued Jairus, "He was surrounded by a great multitude of people. I hesitated but a moment before I pushed my way through the crowd. Upon reaching Him, I fell at

His feet and besought Him greatly, saying, 'Master, my little daughter lieth at the point of death: I pray thee, come and lay thy hands on her, that she may be healed; and she shall live.'"

"That is when He followed you?" questioned Simon.

"Yes," replied Jairus. "But no sooner had we begun our brief sojourn that the Master stopped in the midst of a great crowd and asked who had touched Him?"

Simon appeared confused. "What do you mean, who touched Him?"

Jairus shrugged his shoulders. "We were also perplexed by His question. Even one of His closest followers asked Him, 'Master, the multitude throng thee and press thee, and thou sayest, who touched me?'

"But the Master," continued Jairus, "responded, 'Somebody hath touched me, for I perceive that virtue is gone out of me.'"

By this time Simon was both amazed and yet he was troubled. Who was this Man who claimed to be the Messiah, and whence came His great powers? "What occurred next, Jairus?" inquired Simon, his voice almost pleading.

"It was then that a woman of advanced years slowly, and with much trepidation, came forward and knelt before the Master. She confessed that she had suffered much of her life from a serious affliction, but knew that if she could but touch His robe that she would be healed. The woman then lifted her face to meet the Master's gaze and her eyes were filled with tears, for you see, Simon, upon touching His robe, she felt the sudden and wondrous healing of her body! There was no doubt in her mind but that she had received the blessing she had so desperately sought!"

"And was the Master angered at her actions?" asked Simon.

Jairus shook his head. "Not so. He told the woman, 'Daughter, be of good comfort: thy faith hath made thee whole; go in peace, and be whole of thy plague.'"

Simon suddenly remembered the import of the story. "But what of Leah? Were you not troubled by the delay?"

Jairus thought deeply. "I was at first very worried, Simon. But I then realized that even if Leah died, that He who stood before me could give unto her life once again. Surely He who commands the winds and the waves, and heals the sick, and causes the blind to see and the deaf to hear could give life to my precious daughter once again."

Simon was stunned by Jairus' words! He remained silent, only looking upon his host, but inwardly he was wondering; He who commands the winds and the waves. Could this possibly be the same man whom he had witnessed quiet the raging storm?

"In truth," continued Jairus, "I received word during this time that Leah had in fact passed from this world, but the dreadful news only caused me to implore the Master with greater intensity. There were those who asked that I trouble Him no further since Leah had already died, but He turned to me and graciously said, 'Be not afraid, only believe.'"

"He knew all along the import of your faith," said Simon.

"Yes," said Jairus. "Looking back at it now, I can see why He stopped amidst the crowd. He knew that the woman had touched Him and that she had indeed been healed, but He not only desired to strengthen her faith, but mine as well."

Simon nodded.

"It was not long until we arrived at our humble dwelling. By that time, many had gathered to mourn Leah's death. Miriam was terribly distraught, but upon entering the house, the Master questioned, 'Why make ye this ado, and weep? The damsel is not dead, but sleepeth.' He then requested that only Miriam, myself and three of His disciples accompany Him into the room where Leah lay, the breath of life having left her long ago. He then took her by the hand and commanded, 'Damsel, I say unto thee, arise.' It was with great astonishment and much pleasure that we beheld our dear Leah open her eyes and rise from the bed!"

"Your miracle child," declared Simon, looking at Leah with wonder and amazement.

"Yes," said Jairus, his eyes filled with tears, "our miracle child."

"Did you say that the Messiah was accompanied by three men?" asked Simon, curious about the identity of this good Man.

"Not exactly," said Jairus. "He was accompanied by His twelve disciples, but He requested that only three of them enter the room when He raised Leah from the dead."

"And do you know His name?"

Jairus nodded. "I do. He is known as Jesus. Jesus of Nazareth."

Simon bowed his head and thought to himself, remembering the man who quieted the sea.

"Are you well?" asked Miriam, gazing upon Simon's troubled countenance.

Simon lifted his head and thought to share his experiences on the freighter with them, but he then suddenly beheld the afternoon sun shining through the window. He tenderly looked upon the three before him and said, "I desire more than anything to linger here awhile, but I must continue my journey with haste. Please forgive my sudden departure and accept my sincerest thanks for the many kindnesses you have shown me."

Jairus stood. "No forgiveness is necessary, my young friend. We understand your earnestness. Go with God's watchful care and blessings."

Jairus went to the door and called out to his servant, and within minutes the stallion stood outside the house, well fed and rested.

Simon reluctantly mounted the horse, whereupon Jairus handed him some fresh water and food for his journey. Simon then looked upon Jairus, Miriam and Leah one last time. "Words cannot express my gratitude. I shall never forget you."

He waved farewell and continued his journey south along the Sea of Galilee. He searched the horizon for other riders, but none were to be found. Apparently all had passed him by. It was Wednesday afternoon and already he was more than half a day's journey behind the others.

Chapter Nine

Simon maintained his steady pace in a southerly direction. According to the map, he would soon reach the famed Jordan River which he would follow towards Jericho.

He did not wish to travel at night, but he now had very little choice. For if he limited his travels to daylight hours only, then he surely had no chance of reaching the cave in time. So in his mind he planned a new strategy: henceforth, he would travel continuously, he would simply have to take the risk.

Before long, the sun set over the western horizon, bringing darkness to the desert and making it increasingly difficult for Simon to navigate his way. The stallion was moving slowly, instinctively fearful of what it could not see, but Simon was determined to continue.

He dismounted the animal, grabbed its reigns and led the horse along the dimly lit path. He could see the

Jordan River shimmering in the moonlight off to his left as he walked. Simon continued the journey in such a manner until the sun once again rose the following morning.

It was late Thursday afternoon by the time Simon arrived on the outskirts of the ancient city of Jericho. He had not slept since awakening at the house of Jairus the previous day, but his spirit was buoyed by his progress. For if he continued his present pace, he figured to reach the cave by midnight or shortly thereafter.

He did not, however, relish the forthcoming night-time journey from Jericho to the capital city of Jerusalem. True, it was less than twenty miles in distance, but according to Rachel's uncle, the road was often infested with ruthless bandits who lay in wait for any vulnerable stranger to pass by. They valued life but little and thought nothing of taking it when there was wealth to be gained.

Yet for Simon, there could be no further delays. He figured that the lead riders were even now arriving in Bethlehem and his only chance of joining them was to continue his journey without respite. As he passed through Jericho, he vowed that he would neither eat nor sleep until his advent at the cavern which sheltered Matthias' great wealth.

Simon had not been on the road to Jerusalem for more than an hour when the sun once again descended below the western hills, depriving the desert of its warmth and guiding light. A half-moon lay on the horizon, but much of its illumination was obscured by sporadic clouds. Simon made his way cautiously, his eyes ever watchful for marauding thieves.

It was then that he noticed something peculiar up ahead on the road. He abruptly brought the stallion to a halt and strained to see in the dark. Simon was about to dismount the horse, but thought better of it. Perhaps this was a trap and he wanted to be ready should he have need to flee in haste.

But amidst the dreary darkness and quiet, Simon heard an almost imperceptible groan. He looked about him with great caution and listened for any movement off of the road. He saw and heard nothing unusual and so commanded the horse forward a few steps.

Again he heard a sound of misery, and finally, upon furthering his advance, he beheld the figure of a human being on the road some twenty feet in front of him. Simon dismounted the horse and quickly made his way to the suffering one who had been set upon by robbers.

The brightness of the moon was still dimmed by the clouds, but it shined enough for Simon to see a man laying face down on the road. His clothing had been torn from his body and Simon could see that he had been badly beaten.

Simon slowly rolled the stranger onto his back, and removing his own coat, Simon placed it under the injured man's head. He then gazed at the wounded man and thought his face familiar. Upon further inspection, Simon recognized the victim; it was none other than the Roman soldier who had so arrogantly voiced his disdain for Simon during their meeting at the starting line in Damascus but two days earlier.

Simon was filled with a terrible rage as he looked upon the soldier, and for a brief moment thought of abandoning him. But Simon knew in his heart that he could not possibly leave a brother in such a plight.

Simon quickly built a fire near the side of the road and then carefully moved the soldier near its warming flames. He retrieved his water and poured the cool liquid onto the soldier's dried and bruised lips, after which he set himself to bandaging the Roman's wounds. Simon then unpacked his blanket and covered the soldier against the coolness of the desert air.

As Simon was finishing, the Roman opened his eyes

and beheld Simon bending over him.

"You," faintly cried the soldier. "It is you."

"I did not think that we would see each other again," said Simon as he tightened a bandage around the soldier's arm.

The Roman looked curiously at Simon and shook his head. "Why did you stop? Surely you must realize that the others are by now arriving at the cave."

"Could I leave you here to die?" asked Simon.

"There were others who did, and I am not so sure that I would not leave you."

"I cannot answer for them, or for you. I only know what my God expects of me, and what I expect of myself."

The soldier paused and looked away. "You are a fool."

Simon shrugged his shoulders. "Perhaps."

"By helping me, you have lost all chance of arriving at the cave with the first thousand riders."

Simon sighed. The soldier was right; by morning Matthias' wealth would be gone, the cave emptied of its valued contents. But he knew in his heart that he had to stop.

Simon warily looked about him. "We shall wait here but a few hours and allow your wounds to cease their bleeding, then we shall continue onto Jerusalem. I fear that the thieves might return if we delay our journey much longer."

The soldier simply nodded, but his soul was racked with torment and guilt. No matter how gruff or calloused he appeared to be, his heart was warmed by the kindness and mercy of this young man whom he had, at one time, so gravely offended. "Tell me, what is your name and from whence do you hail?"

Simon raised the soldier's head and gave him some water to drink. "I am Simon, and come from the city of Cyrene which borders the Great Sea."

The soldier slowly sipped the water, after which

Simon lowered his head back onto the coat.

"I am Claudius, and come from Rome, but am presently serving in Judea."

Simon nodded.

"Such a great distance and hardship you have endured, Simon. Can wealth be so important that you risk your life in such a manner?"

"I have never viewed it as such. I have a young family to care for and thought the wealth to be a means of supporting them."

Claudius bowed his head and closed his eyes in shame. This young man before him had sacrificed his opportunity for wealth so that he might aid a brother. And the wealth was not being sought for the purchase of luxuries, rather it was to support the simple wants and needs of his young family.

But Claudius would not allow it. With some exerted effort, he slowly rose to a sitting position. "Simon, you must leave at once!" he implored. "There is yet time for you to arrive at the cave while the wealth remains! But you must make haste! "

Simon gently grasped the soldier by the arms and lowered him back to the ground. "Calm yourself, my friend. You must not move for several hours or else the bleeding shall not cease. Do not concern yourself with my humble circumstances. All shall be well."

Simon's words and expressions revealed no regrets, but inside his heart was aching. He had desperately hoped to share in Matthias' wealth, but that possibility now seemed all but hopeless.

Claudius, however, was just as stubborn. "Simon, you cannot remain here a moment longer. Believe me, my life has little value. Surely the earth will not suffer if I am left here to die. I have no family, and have spent my life only appeasing my riotous desires. But you have a family to care for. Please, Simon, go now. I relieve you of any obligation you may feel towards me."

Simon smiled at his newfound friend. "I appreciate

your feelings, but nothing you say will change my decision. I cannot leave you, and that is final."

Claudius nodded in surrender. "Very well, Simon. So be it. But it is my hope that you are one day rewarded for your kindness."

"Your change of heart is payment enough for me," said Simon, rising to tend to his horse.

Claudius weakly laughed. "I suppose it is Simon. I suppose it is."

It was later that night, as Simon sat near the fire keeping a constant vigil over the sleeping soldier, that he heard a faint noise in the distance. He quietly rose and walked in the direction from whence came the sound. He patrolled the area for several minutes and found himself a good distance from the fire. His search, however, revealed nothing.

But as he looked back upon the camp, he discovered the object of his exploration, for there, rummaging through his pack, was a thief, a knife hung at his side. Apparently the robber had assumed Claudius to be the owner of the horse and sole occupant of the camp. He had no knowledge of Simon's existence.

Simon approached the camp with stealth, his heart pounding in his chest. He hid behind a large rock and from there observed the bandit. It was Simon's hope that the robber would simply take what little money was in the pack and leave in peace.

It was then that the bandit walked over to Claudius, who lay sleeping near the fire, and withdrew his knife! Simon began to tremble and sweat gathered on his forehead. He took a deep breath and began to move towards the thief. The robber, however, apparently considered Claudius to be no serious threat, and so returned the knife to its sheath. Simon closed his eyes in relief and retreated to his hidden fortress.

The thief then retraced his steps back to the horse and prepared to mount it. Simon suddenly froze. "He is taking the stallion!" For some reason it had never occurred to Simon that the robber would make off with the animal. He was not prepared for this.

Simon was more than willing to part with the money, for he certainly placed greater value upon his life than the few pence that remained in the leather pouch. But he could not, and would not, permit the theft of the stallion. It would be different if he were alone, for he would simply allow the bandit to take the horse and then Simon would easily walk the remaining distance to Jerusalem. But what of Claudius? Simon could not carry him, and he would surely die if stranded in the desert.

Simon swallowed hard and tried to think. He was not a coward, but never before had he faced such danger, and yet there was little time for contemplation. The thief had paused for a moment to retrieve a few coins which had dropped to the ground and Simon, sensing an opportunity, did not hesitate. Hoping to surprise the bandit, Simon ran towards him, screaming as loudly as he could! The noise awoke Claudius and he suddenly rose to a sitting position.

Shocked, the thief turned to see Simon running towards him. Simon carried only a large stick, but amidst the commotion and darkness of the night, the thief thought it to be a sword. He then turned to see the awakened Claudius, and figuring that he was suddenly out numbered, the robber fled into the still blackness of the night.

Simon and Claudius embraced, awkwardly laughing their relief, but there was no time for celebration. The frightful incident had taught them a lesson; their journey must be continued at once.

Simon helped Claudius mount the horse and then took the stallion by the reigns and led it off into the night. With any luck they would be in Jerusalem by sunrise the following day.

It was early Friday morning when Simon and

Claudius arrived in the small town of Bethany, which lies on the highway from Jericho, only a mile or so east of Jerusalem.

Simon had planned on continuing his journey with Claudius until they had reached the capital, but the Roman was now far too weak to endure such a sojourn. He barely held his position on the horse and rode in an almost unconscious stupor.

Simon located a small inn within the town and led the stallion to its front porch. He then carefully reached up and helped Claudius dismount the animal, placing the Roman's left arm around his shoulders. A young man attending the inn saw their plight and hastened outside to assist them.

"May I be of service to you?" asked the young man, speaking to Simon.

"My sincerest thanks. Would you please help me take this man into one of your rooms. He has been badly injured and requires the attention of a doctor."

"Most assuredly, sir," replied the young man as he raced to Claudius' side.

As they entered the inn, the young man pointed to a room only a few doors down the hall. "We shall place him there, after which I shall bring the doctor."

Simon and the young man carefully lowered Claudius to the bed. The soldier was speaking, but his words were confused and carried little meaning.

"Calm yourself," said Simon. "All shall be well, good friend."

The doctor arrived within minutes and sat beside his patient on the bed. Simon occupied a chair not far away. His expression revealed his concern.

After several minutes of examination, the doctor turned to Simon. "You are his friend?"

Simon nodded. "I am."

The doctor stood and stretched his back. "Well, you have little to worry about. He has been bruised and has lost a goodly amount of blood, but he has suffered nothing that a few days of rest and proper food will not take care of."

Simon beamed his delight. He turned to the young man and said, "I must depart and continue my journey towards Bethlehem, and I humbly ask that you care for my good friend. Take this . . ," Simon took from his pocket two pence and gave them to his host, ". . . and whatsoever you spend more, I shall come again and repay you."

The young man accepted the coins, but gestured to Simon, "Be not concerned, sir. What you have paid shall easily suffice. Give no troubled thought for your friend. I shall surely care for him until he is fully recovered."

Simon grasped the young innkeeper by his shoulders. "May the God of Heaven bless you for your kindness."

It was the doctor who next spoke. "What, may I ask, draws you from us with such haste?"

Simon looked directly at the doctor. "The race!"

"The race?! Then you must depart now!" commanded the physician, pushing Simon out of the room. "Do not delay a moment longer! There were many riders who passed through Bethany just last night."

Simon grasped the doctor by the hand. "I realize that I have fallen behind, but I must continue, for their still exists a small chance that some wealth yet remains."

The doctor agreed. "Yes! Yes! Of course you must continue! For how can you travel as far as you have without knowing for certain what awaits you at the cave? Take the highway into Jerusalem and thence follow the road south to the city of David."

Simon gestured his gratitude one last time and then turned to leave, the proximity of the cave seemed to lift his spirit. He mounted the stallion and quickly headed west. He hoped to arrive at the cave in less than an hour!

Chapter Ten

The highway from Bethany passes just south of the summit of the Mount of Olives, where the road descends into the Kidron Valley, before rising once again to the eastern wall surrounding the city of Jerusalem.

Simon was riding with great haste, but suddenly stopped his advance when he arrived at the road's highest point. There, before him, across the small ravine, was the famed city of his ancestors, and within it's walls majestically stood the Temple, the spiritual emblem of all Judea.

Had it been another time and under different circumstances, Simon would have lingered a greater while, but after pausing only a moment, he descended into the Kidron and then made his way up the steep ascent until he entered one of the eastern portals of Jerusalem.

The city was glutted with humanity, for many had

come to celebrate the sacred festivities of the Passover. Simon dismounted the stallion and with great care led it through the turbulent masses. The stench of burnt animal sacrifices filled the air. The road leading to Bethlehem departed the city's western gate, thus Simon was forced to transverse the excited multitude before he could continue his journey.

But as he attempted to pass by one of the northern gates, Simon met a large throng which for some reason had gathered along both sides of the road. It appeared as if they had assembled to pay homage to a person of prominence, and out of curiosity, and because he could not make his way through the restless crowd, Simon ceased his journey to see who this person might be.

But after mingling amidst the throng for a moment, Simon noticed something most eerie and strange about these people, for some were shouting obscenities, while others wept openly and mourned. It was indeed a rare mixture of emotions displayed by the multitude.

It was not long until the procession began to pass by; first came the Roman soldiers, followed by Caiaphas, the High Priest, in all his royal garb. It was then that Simon noticed Him; a Man in tattered clothing, carrying a cross, and upon His head had been thrust a crown of thorns, while His bare back revealed the wounds suffered from a merciless scourging. That is when Simon recognized Him; it was He who had calmed the raging tempest but a week earlier!

Simon turned to a man who stood next to him and pleaded, "Please, sir, tell me what terrible deed this good Man has committed to warrant such a fate."

The man angrily turned to Simon with hate in his eyes. "Why do you call Him good? Have you not heard?" he questioned indignantly. "He is the Nazarene who claims to be the Promised Messiah and the Son of God!" The man then returned his attention back to the procession and joined the maddening shouts of the crowd. "Crucify him! Crucify Jesus of Nazareth!"

Simon could not move! For the irate onlooker had answered the very question that had troubled him since his meeting with Jairus; the Stranger on the ship and the Galilean Prophet who claimed to be the Messiah were indeed the same Man.

Pushing people aside, Simon struggled with all his might to make his way through the crazed throng until he stood at the side of the road where the Nazarene was passing. It was then that Jesus dropped to the ground from the weight of the cross and had difficulty in rising. The guards hesitated a moment, but then tired of His respite, and showing Him no mercy, began to whip Him.

It soon became obvious to all that the Nazarene, weakened through His previous torture and suffering, could no longer bear the horrifying instrument of His death. The guards hastily looked into the crowd, and observing Simon standing nearby, grabbed him by the arm and forced him into their service.

Simon, seeing no way of refusing the soldiers' dreadful command, reluctantly stepped forward and tenderly removed the cross from Jesus' weakened body. As he did so, Jesus looked up and gazed into Simon's eyes.

"I am so sorry," whispered Simon. "How I wish that this action were forced upon another."

Jesus could do little more than faintly nod His understanding.

They continued further up the mount called Calvary, when Simon also slipped and fell, the cross landing on top of him. He was momentarily dazed and did not rise quickly enough for the guards who followed after him.

"Get up on your feet, you hideous dog!" one of them yelled as he stepped forward and maliciously flung his whip across Simon's back and shoulders. Feeling the searing pain as the whip tore into his flesh, Simon quickly rose to his feet and continued the march until he reached the top of the knoll. There, the cross was taken from him by the soldiers and placed upon the ground.

Simon gazed upon the harrowing scene and beheld the Nazarene; His suffering was obvious as He stooped forward, hands upon His knees, yet He mourned not once. It was as if He had accepted this dreadful lot and was resigned to such a fate. The soldiers removed from Him His tattered raiment so that He stood before the crowd naked, after which they placed upon Him a small loin cloth. They offered Him a drink, a narcotic to deaden His senses and lessen His physical suffering upon the cross, but He refused it.

Simon winced as the executioners proceeded with their dreadful task, mercilessly driving nails into the Nazarene's quivering palms and feet. The cross was then stood upright and secured between two others.

Simon, desiring to rid himself of the attention he had drawn through his forced participation, slowly retreated from the cross and joined with the others who had gathered to mourn their Master's death.

The majority of the crowd, however, wasted little time in reviling Him. Their defiance grew bolder now that the object of their loathing hung suffering before them.

"If He be the Son of God, then surely He can save Himself!"

"If He comes down from the cross, then we will believe that He is the Christ!"

The Nazarene was forced to endure such verbal taunts for the first hour, but through it all He remained dignified and silent, excepting for one expression of unforgettable divine mercy which caused Simon to marvel all the further, "Forgive them, Father, for they know not what they do."

It was during the second hour that Simon observed

a man slowly making his way to the cross. It was John, he whom Simon had seen on the Phoenician ship. Beside him stood a woman, weeping as she looked upon the Nazarene. Jesus' words revealed that the distraught woman was His mother.

Jesus looked upon Mary from the cross, and with a tender heart, commended her earthly care and protection to His beloved disciple, saying, "Woman, behold thy son." And to John, He said, "Behold thy mother." The apostle then lead the grieving Mary away from the heart-wrenching scene.

About the third hour a strange and eerie mist enveloped the land. The troubled multitude vainly attempted to ignore its meaning and feigned little concern, but Simon discerned by the frightened expression on their faces that they were deeply worried by the unusual darkness.

It was then that a cry of deep distress issued from the central cross! It was the Christ. His cry, however, was not one of physical pain, but rather a heaven-directed plea understood by few. "My God, my God, why hast thou forsaken me?"

As Simon looked upon the dying Nazarene, he knew then, nothing doubting, that He who hung before him was indeed what He claimed to be. And Simon finally began to understand, even in a small way, just how the Savior of mankind could possibly comprehend and feel within His own soul the sorrows and trials of others. For it appeared to Simon that the Messiah was suffering under a greater burden than what even His tremendous physical torture should have brought upon Him. He truly seemed to be carrying a weight upon His shoulders which no one had ever before suffered with, and which no one would surely ever suffer from again. Of that Simon was certain.

Sometime during the sixth hour, after the feelings of abandonment had passed, the Savior gazed down from the cross and uttered His one expression of physical suffering. "I thirst," He said. Perhaps it was fear of the soldiers who guarded the cross, or the threatening presence of Caiaphas that caused the lack of response to the Lord's gentle plea. Simon, however, hesitated but a moment before he stepped forward, and grabbing a reed which had attached to it a small sponge, he dipped it into a vessel of water and pressed it against the Savior's parched and wanting lips.

The Savior then fixed His gaze upon Simon and even amidst His great suffering managed a faint, warm smile, which Simon would always carry in his heart.

The Savior then cried out, "It is finished! Father, into thy hands I commend my spirit." He let out one last cry of severe anguish, then bowed His head and breathed His last mortal breath. The Savior of the world was dead!

At that very moment, the earth shook violently and a terrible storm arose. It was as if the earth itself was mourning the death of the Messiah, and so impressed was the Roman centurion who kept the vigil at the cross that he vocally proclaimed, "Truly, this was the Son of God!"

As tears mingled with rain upon his face, Simon walked to the foot of the cross where the soldier stood, and gazing upon the lifeless body, he voiced his agreement with the Roman, saying, "It is so. Truly, He was the Son of God!"

Sometime thereafter, when much of the crowd had descended the knoll, two men of prominence, one named Nicodemus, a member of the Sanhedrin, and the other, Joseph of Arimathea, carefully removed the Savior's body from the cross and carried Him to a garden tomb, hewn in the rock not far from the knoll. A group of mourning and distraught women also followed. Simon observed from afar, not wanting to intrude upon those who now desired to express their loving devotion to their Master one last time.

Once they had entered the tomb, Joseph and

Nicodemus reverently cleansed the body and anointed it with myrrh and aloes, after which they wrapped the Lord's body in clean linen, but because of the approaching Jewish Sabbath the interment had to be made with haste. Their service complete, the two men secured the sepulchre by rolling a large stone over its opening.

Soon darkness completely covered the land and Simon, having no place to go, was left alone on a small hill overlooking the tomb. He had not slept since departing Jairus' house two days earlier and exhaustion now overcame him. He laid down upon the ground under a small rock overhang which shielded him against the storm. All thoughts of the race had left his mind.

He turned over onto his side and felt the searing pain of the wound caused by the Roman's whip and tears flowed freely from his eyes. It was not the pain, however, that caused his emotions, rather it was the vivid scene of a just and honorable Man falsely accused, sorely mistreated and suffering such terrible atrocities.

His weariness, however, finally overcame him and he closed his eyes and fell into a restless slumber. Because of his tremendous fatigue he would sleep through the morrow and not awake until the following day.

It was early Sunday morning, just before sunrise, while darkness still covered the land, that Simon was awakened by a radiant light, and at the same moment he felt the earth tremble mightily beneath him. Shocked, he hastily arose and gazed down towards the portal of the tomb from whence the light emanated. There, to his surprise, sat a man whose countenance was most brilliant, and whose robe shone as white as the sun at noon day.

The angel sat upon the massive stone which at one time had covered the opening to the sepulcher, but which now had been miraculously rolled back.

Simon was filled with awe and bewilderment, but for some reason he felt no fear or panic. It was then that the sun fully rose and Simon, hearing footsteps from the path below which lead to the garden, turned to see the same devout and faithful women who had witnessed the burial two days earlier, once again returning to the sepulcher bearing spices and ointments for the further anointing of Jesus' body.

As they reached the tomb, they also beheld the angel and were much afraid, but the heavenly visitor calmed them, saying, "Fear not ye: for I know that ye seek Jesus, who was crucified. He is not here: for he is risen, as he said. Come, see the place where the Lord lay. And go quickly, and tell his disciples that he is risen from the dead; and behold, he goeth before you into Galilee; there shall ye see him; lo, I have told you."

After gazing into the tomb, the women left in a wondering panic, but Simon remained, observing from afar. Having delivered his message, the angel also departed. Simon's mind was racing as he attempted to comprehend the divine messenger's words: "He is not here; he is risen." He slowly descended the small hill and approached the entrance to the tomb and gazed therein. It was empty! The only remnant of testimony to the Lord's death was the linen which had at one time covered His body.

Confused and mystified, Simon exited the tomb and returned to his place of solitude on the hill. Shortly thereafter, the sound of voices caught his attention and he turned to behold one of the women who had earlier been present during the angelic visitation returning in haste, while before her ran two men. One of them was John, and the other Simon recognized from his journey on the Phoenician freighter. The two disciples entered the tomb, remained but a moment, and then departed, but the woman lingered, weeping for the loss of her Master.

It was then that the woman and Simon, still witnessing from afar, became aware of the presence of another man. Simon thought it odd that he had not seen the stranger draw nigh unto the sepulchre. He approached the sorrowful woman near the tomb and inquired, "Woman, why weepest thou? Whom seekest thou?"

The grieved woman scarcely lifted her tear-stained face to look upon the man, but supposing him to be the caretaker of the garden, and assuming that he would have knowledge of where the body of her Lord was, said, "Sir, if thou hast borne him hence, tell me where thou hast laid him, and I will take him away."

The man tenderly said unto her, "Mary."

She paused, for there was something so very familiar in his kind and caring tone. No further verbal expression was necessary. She lifted her gaze and beheld her Lord!

"This cannot be!" cried Simon under his breath. "It is He! It is Jesus!"

Mary impulsively reached out to Him, saying, "My Beloved Master!"

But the Lord gently restrained her, saying, "Touch me not; for I am not yet ascended to my Father, but go to my brethren, and say unto them, I ascend unto my Father, and your Father; and to my God, and your God."

Mary bowed and obeyed immediately. In an instant the Savior was also gone, leaving Simon, once again, alone unto himself.

But what was he to do? Where was he to go? He had witnessed so much; events that would change his life forever. More than anything he desired to follow after the two disciples into Galilee, but such would be an impossibility.

At that moment, Simon looked down the path to the portal from whence the procession had exited the city and there, to his surprise, stood the stallion.

It had faithfully remained, waiting for Simon. For the first time in two days Simon's thoughts returned to the race and to those for whom he labored; his beloved Rachel and Rebecca. And still he bore a responsibility and obligation to Jacob, one which he did not take lightly.

It was less than six miles to the cave, and although he knew that the wealth must now be exhausted, inwardly he felt something drawing him to the cavern. Perhaps, by divine province, a portion of the wealth somehow remained.

He mounted the horse, and locating the road to Bethlehem, he began the last leg of his journey. After he had traveled a short distance, Simon gazed back towards Jerusalem. There, rising above the horizon, stood the skull-like knoll called Golgotha, still bearing the three crosses, and off to its right was the garden tomb. Simon would never forget either of them, and he longed to share with Rachel the wonderful events which he had witnessed. But first, he had one more journey to make. A brief journey to a cave in Bethlehem.

Chapter Eleven

Simon felt newfound enthusiasm as he approached the cave. He threw himself from the stallion even before it had completely halted, and ran into the massive cavern.

Once therein, Simon quickly glanced about him, but what he saw caused the blood to run from his head; there were only empty chests strewn about the ground, which at one time had contained the great merchant's wealth.

Simon frantically rummaged through the cave, searching through the overturned chests, hoping with all his soul. But finally he resigned himself to his sure fate; he had arrived too late and the wealth was gone. Simon despondently sat on one of the barren chests and dropped his head into his hands. Once again he had failed. What would he tell Rachel? How could he face her bearing such disappointing news? It was as if someone had thrust a dagger through his aching heart.

Amidst his sorrow, Simon did not notice the man enter the cave. "I am Demetrius, servant of Matthias. Are you amongst those who sought the master's wealth?"

Startled, Simon raised his head and then stood quickly. "Yes . . . yes, I rode in the great race."

Demetrius looked confused, and tilting his head slightly to the right, he stared at Simon. "The last of the riders arrived Friday at the setting of the sun, and the wealth had been distributed by noon of that same day."

"Then the wealth is indeed gone?" inquired Simon, knowing the answer before he asked.

Demetrius nodded and pointed to the empty chests. "It grieves me to say that it is. As you can see, none of the wealth remains."

Exhausted, disappointed and confused, Simon slowly sat back down on the chest. He had not anticipated such a dreary conclusion to his journey.

Demetrius approached him, saying, "I am most curious, young man, as to why you arrived so much later than the others?"

"Forgive me, sir, but does it truly matter?" asked Simon.

"Perhaps not," said Demetrius, shrugging his shoulders, "but I would very much like to know the reason for your delay."

Simon paused, what harm could it bring? He then recounted the events of his journey, and as he did so, the man's eyes began to fill with wonder. He gazed at Simon as if he were a friend, lost years ago, but now found.

When Simon had finished relating the story of his travels, Demetrius patted him on the shoulder. "Tell me, young man, what is your name?"

"I am Simon, from Cyrene."

"You have sojourned a great distance."

"But for naught, I fear."

"Do you have family?" asked Demetrius.

"A wife and a daughter, and we are expecting our second child in the coming summer."

"And it is for them that you sought this wealth?"

Simon dejectedly nodded. His eyes were moist.

Demetrius then looked upon Simon with great concern. "Before you depart this day, shall you not sup with me, young Simon? I am most certain that you have not eaten well for days."

Simon stood. "I am indeed most grateful for your kindness, Demetrius. I have no money and still a great journey awaits me as I return to Cyrene. I would surely savor a good meal."

"It is well, young friend. Follow me and we shall indeed enjoy the feast of a king."

It was but a few moments later that Demetrius escorted a disheartened Simon through a gate which lead to a beautiful, but unpretentious estate. The grounds were simple, but well kept and pleasant. And the house, which rested towards the back of the estate, was modest in size, yet splendid to behold.

Simon entered the house and was escorted down a long corridor, the lighting seemed to dim the further they walked. Demetrius slowed his pace and then stopped in front of a large cedar door, whereupon he quietly knocked, opened the door and then entered, gesturing for Simon to follow.

Upon entering the room, however, Simon was perplexed, for instead of the dining hall, they had entered a large bed chamber, and before him, in the faintest of light, lay an old, feeble man. His eyes were closed.

Demetrius turned to Simon and whispered, "Please, remain here but a moment."

"But what . . ."

"All shall be explained in time. Now please, remain here," pleaded Demetrius.

74

"I shall do as you ask," replied Simon.

Demetrius then made his way to the side of the bed where the old man lay and gently patted his shoulder, saying, "Sire, he is here. It is he. His name is Simon and he hails from Cyrene."

The old man opened his eyes and struggled to sit up as Demetrius propped up a pillow behind him. The old man then slowly turned and retrieved a goblet from the small table near his bed and sipped gently from the cup, after which he returned the goblet to the table. He then focused his gaze upon Simon and smiled weakly. "Demetrius, bid him come forward that he may sit next to me," commanded the old man.

Demetrius obeyed. "Simon, the master bids you to come forward."

Simon reluctantly moved closer, but nothing had been said or done to settle his confusion.

The old man looked kindly at Simon, patted the bed next to him and asked, "Please, my son, will you not sit on the bed next to me?"

Once again, Simon obeyed and sat next to the old man, who then gently took Simon's hand in his while gazing into his eyes. Simon's heart almost ceased to beat when he figured the identity of the old man.

"Matthias?" he whispered.

The old man nodded. "It is I, my dear friend." His voice was raspy and barely audible. "You are surprised to see me, young Simon?"

Simon began to stammer. "Well . . . yes. I thought that . . . you were . . ."

"Dead?" interrupted Matthias.

Simon bowed his head. "That is what we were told."

"The announcement of my death was no fabrication, my friend. It was only proclaimed prematurely. As you can see, this mortal body shall soon return to the dust of the earth from which it was made."

Matthias gazed intently at Simon. "I realize that you must have many questions, Simon, but before we can proceed, I must insist that you share with me the details of your journey which brought you to the cave."

Simon's confusion had only been enhanced, but just as he had done with Demetrius, he recounted the entire story of his journey to Matthias - the quieting of the storm, the race, Jairus and his family, Claudius, and lastly, the Messiah.

When Simon had finished, the old man closed his eyes and sighed deeply, his relief and pleasure were obvious. He then turned to his loyal servant and said, "Demetrius, once again your service to me has been most invaluable. He is indeed the one we have sought and waited for. I express to you my sincerest gratitude. Please, leave us now, that I may speak with Simon alone."

Demetrius humbly bowed before Matthias. "As you wish, sire. Call if you have need of me."

"I shall, good friend."

Once the door had closed, Matthias turned to the startled and shaken Simon. "Be at peace, my young friend. All shall be explained to you in good time." The old man paused and looked kindly at Simon. "Tell me, my son, why did you journey such a great distance to participate in the race?"

Simon looked into Matthias' old, but benevolent eyes. "I have a young wife and family to care for, unfortunately my efforts to provide for them have been most unfruitful."

"In what business do you labor, Simon?"

"I once sold wares door to door and at our local market in Cyrene."

Matthias grinned. "A fellow merchant!"

"Our only semblance, I fear," said a dejected Simon.

"Your efforts have not born much success?" asked Matthias.

"No, sire."

"Adversity, challenge and discouragement are not easily swallowed are they?" said the great merchant, looking tenderly upon Simon's disfigured face.

Simon looked at the old man and simply shook his head. A tear fell down his cheek.

Matthias sighed heavily and patted Simon's hand. "Unfortunately, there are very few who escape such trials and hardships in this life . . . including myself."

Simon appeared surprised. "But you are the most successful merchant in all of . . ."

Matthias raised his hand into the air and quieted Simon. "Perhaps it is time that I share with you the reason that you are here."

Simon nodded and the old man sank back into his pillow and began his story. . . .

Chapter Twelve

"It was many years ago, Simon, that my parents departed Judea and settled in Damascus where I was brought into this world. It was there that I met my dear wife and where I commenced my labors as a merchant. In time, we returned to Judea and made our home in Bethlehem where our three wonderful children were born."

Simon could see tears forming in Matthias' aged eyes.

"I struggled in business for years, facing many discouragements, and was able to provide but a meager existence for my family. Yet even amidst our humble circumstances, we were happy and felt blessed to have each other. It was then that I was confronted with my greatest trial of all; a terrible plague swept through Judea, taking the lives of many. My house, tragically, was not spared; my wife and children died within a matter of weeks."

"I am so sorry," whispered Simon.

The old man could feel that Simon's words of solace were sincere and he nodded his gratitude.

"It was the deepest and darkest days of my entire life," continued Matthias. "My business, what little there was, fell into ruins, and I began to drink heavily, attempting to forget my sorrows. I felt that I had nothing to live for and so one day I decided to end my life."

Simon sat staring at the old man. He could not believe what he was hearing.

"One night, I departed my humble abode and commenced by brief sojourn to the outskirts of the city where I had decided to take my miserable life. I had little difficulty in seeing my way, for a bright star, one which I had never before seen, shone brilliantly from the heavens."

"A new star?" questioned Simon.

"Yes," answered Matthias. "It was very strange, very strange indeed. In any regard, I finally arrived at my specified destination where I had planned to end my life, and was about to do so, when three strangers traveling from the east crossed my path. I was startled, as were they, and upon their pleading, I ceased my endeavors."

"They saved your life," said Simon.

"It is true, but they feared to leave me to myself, so one of them asked that I accompany them on an important errand, after which he desired to visit with me, hoping to help me."

"And you journeyed with them?" asked Simon.

"It is so. I rode with one of the travelers, Ezakar by name, and as we made our way, he asked me of my plight and the reasons I desired to take my life. I told him of my family and the many discouragements and hardships which I had faced. But before long we arrived at their destination."

Simon curiously stared at Matthias.

"It was a lowly stable located in back of one of the town's inns. The three men dismounted their animals and removed what appeared to be precious gifts from their packs. Ezakar then turned to me and requested that I wait for him, saying that he would return momentarily. I promised that I would obey."

"For what reason did they bear such precious gifts to a stable?" asked Simon.

"I was not certain at first, but as I gazed further into the stable, I beheld a beautiful young woman who tenderly held a small babe in her arms, while her husband protectively stood nearby. The three men approached the infant and knelt before him. It was then that I saw Ezakar gaze back at me as if he were deciding an important issue in his mind."

"What do you mean?" asked Simon.

"As the other two men were placing their treasures near the mother and the child, Ezakar returned one of his gifts, a small scroll, to the pouch which hung at his side."

Simon stirred. "Who was the young child, and why should the three men travel so great a distance to bring him gifts?"

"As the three men left the stable, I asked of them the same question. Ezakar turned to me and bade me never to forget, for the child within the stable was none other than the Promised Messiah . . . the Son of God."

"The Promised Messiah?!" cried Simon. "The Same whom I witnessed die on the cross?"

The old man reverently nodded his head. "It was He, Simon."

Simon attempted to subdue his astonishment. "Please, continue sire."

"It is well. After returning to my humble abode, Ezakar kindly visited with me the entire night, attempting to brighten my spirit. Before he departed the following morning, he retrieved the tiny scroll from his pack and gave it to me. He informed me that it contained a sacred message of hope and inspiration which had been divinely revealed from on high to a mighty prophet who had labored amongst his ancestors in the east many centuries ago. The message had been carefully preserved and passed down from generation to generation.

"Ezakar then told me that he had learned from an angel that the Chosen Messiah was to be born in the town of Bethlehem, and was instructed, along with his two fellow-servants, to follow the star until they had reached the birthplace of the Savior. The three men were also commanded to bring unto the Child precious gifts, and Ezakar, knowing of the tremendous sorrows and trials that the Messiah would surely face as He performed His great mission, was hopeful that the revealed message might be of some help to Him. Ezakar, therefore, transcribed the sacred words onto the scroll and carried it from the east along with the other treasures intended for the Infant."

"And yet Ezakar withheld it from Him and bequeathed it unto you." proclaimed Simon.

"It is so. Ezakar informed me that the Savior would not have need of the scroll until He was thirty years of age, at which time He would commence His ministry. Ezakar told me that he would allow me to use the scroll and benefit from its message only with the condition that I return it to the true Beneficiary when the time came. I covenanted that I would do so."

"And through the years you retained and utilized the scroll?" inquired Simon.

"Yes," answered the aged Matthias. "As instructed, I read it every day. Its divine message is one of hope, encouragement and inspiration and renders unto its reader the power to continue life's battle even in the face of hardship, struggle, discouragement and despair, something we all face from time to time to one degree or another."

Simon weakly nodded, for he knew well of what the

81

great merchant spoke.

"The scroll," continued Matthias, "has helped and inspired me to persist through my struggles and achieve the fulfillment, happiness, and peace of mind which I have enjoyed during my earthly sojourn."

"And in time you returned the scroll to the Messiah?" asked Simon.

"That is correct. I attempted to keep in contact with the young family, but lost track of them when they departed for Egypt to escape the murderous plot of King Herod. It was then that I fully comprehended the reason why Ezakar was instructed to bear treasures unto them, for it was with this wealth that they were able to sustain themselves while they tarried in Egypt. I later discovered that they had settled in the small town of Nazareth in Galilee.

"It was many years later that I once again heard of Him. There was talk of a great prophet teaching in the wilderness beyond Jordan, and I calculated that the Messiah would now be thirty years of age and ready to commence His great work. I journeyed to see the prophet, but did not find the Messiah. Instead, I found the forerunner known as the Baptist, he who was to prepare the Messiah's way. It was to be yet another six months before I finally met the Promised One."

"And you gave Him the scroll?" asked Simon.

"Yes. I learned that He was abiding in Bethany, not too far distant from here, and so I hastened to see Him. I entered the dwelling and asked to speak with Him, and He graciously accepted as if He were expecting me. I presented Him with the scroll and informed Him of its origin. Upon inspecting it, He clutched it to His chest, for He truly understood its worth. He thanked me and said that He would indeed treasure the gift and that it would surely be a source of strength, not only to Him, but more so to His faithful followers. I then returned to my home here in Bethlehem."

Simon breathed deeply and sighed. "Such a mar-velous story, sire."

"It is."

"But sire," said Simon, "I am yet puzzled as to why I am here."

"Of course, young Simon. You must forgive my forgetfulness," pleaded Matthias. "About three months ago I learned that I was suffering from a serious illness, one that would take my life, and so I prepared to leave this mortal world in peace. I made plans to dispense the majority of my wealth to the poor, and I also decided to bequeath my estate and the remainder of my riches to my servant, Demetrius, for his kindness and loyalty so thoughtfully displayed these many years.

"I had finally made the necessary preparations for my mortal departure, after which time I remained on the estate, living the remainder of my days in peace, expecting my life's work to be complete. But my plans were suddenly altered when the Messiah came to visit me."

"The Messiah came here?" asked Simon, now more bewildered than ever.

"Yes," said Matthias. "Not but six weeks ago."

"And what was the purpose of His visit?" asked Simon.

"Once again, He expressed His gratitude for the scroll, but He informed me that He would have no further need of it. And since I had originally given it to Him, He thought it best that He return the scroll to me and that I be the one to find a worthy and needful recipient to give it to."

"He knew that He was going to die," Simon declared softly, suddenly recalling and comprehending the Savior's words to His apostles before departing the Phoenician freighter.

"It is so," replied Matthias. "He informed me that His time had indeed arrived to drink that bitter cup given Him by His Father. But before He departed my humble dwelling, He asked me something that greatly surprised me."

Simon leaned closer to the old man.

"He asked me if I desired to be healed from my affliction."

"And yet you are still sorely afflicted, are you not?" questioned Simon.

Matthias slowly nodded his head. "It is so. For you see, before I answered, He said that He thought it only just that He inform me that my dear family was anxiously awaiting my return in His eternal kingdom. It did not take me long before I realized that my true desire was to once again be with them."

Simon looked into the old man's eyes; they were now filled with tears.

"The Master understood," continued Matthias, "and withheld His healing hand from me. But He embraced me and filled my soul with a comfort that is both endless and timeless. As He stood to take His leave, He turned one last time and said, 'Fear not, Matthias, for we shall soon meet again in the peaceful courts above where the true crown of glory and honor awaits.'"

Matthias humbly bowed his head, but then raised it to the heavens while calmly proclaiming, "It is there that He has gone, and it is there that I shall soon follow." There was a short pause and Matthias began to sob quietly as he whispered, "Oh, how wonderful it shall be to hold my dear wife and children once again."

The shared events had drained Simon, but after a long moment of silence, he asked, "Please, sire, can you now tell me why I am here?"

The old man nodded and faintly smiled. "Of course, my friend. After the Savior departed, I immediately summoned Demetrius and informed him of my assigned duty; that of finding the one whom the heavens had ordained to receive the scroll's divine message. We worked arduously for days to conceive a means whereby we could find the worthy heir. I felt my strength leaving me and thought I would surely fail in my task, when I was suddenly inspired from on high with an idea."

Simon sat up and moved ever closer to Matthias. "The race!"

The old man patted Simon on the hand. "It is so, my good friend. The race was the answer. For this reason I announced my death prematurely and the plans to distribute my remaining wealth at the conclusion of the race. I knew that it would indeed be sufficient reason to draw many of our people to the cave. I felt strongly in my heart that the God of Heaven would guide my soul and help Demetrius and I choose the one who was deemed worthy to receive the divine scroll."

Simon sat quietly, staring into the aged eyes of the great merchant who sat before him. Even then, Matthias' breathing was labored.

"Both Demetrius and I became most concerned, however, when after the conclusion of the race we still had not found the one we sought." Matthias then gently squeezed Simon's trembling hand. "But that is when you arrived, and after learning of your journey I am quite convinced that you are the one we have patiently awaited."

Simon swallowed. "Me?"

"It is so," declared Matthias. "I realize how badly you wanted to win your share of wealth, but still you were willing to sacrifice riches to aid your fellow man. Such an act speaks highly of your character and worthiness. And I dare not ignore your unforgettable experiences with the Messiah. Surely these are not mere coincidences, but rather unmistakable signs from above. The wound on your back which you received while bearing His cross is a testament of itself.

"But this is not all, young Simon. My soul is at peace for the first time since I received this errand from the Lord. The tranquility which I now enjoy proves to me that you are the one which I have sought."

Simon was speechless. He neither moved nor spoke.

Matthias then reached towards the wooden chest near the side of his bed, and with some effort, opened it, and from it he removed a small scroll. Simon observed the pain-staking movements with awe. Matthias placed the tiny scroll on his lap and then attempted to comfortably situate himself on the pillows which bore his upper body. Having done so, he turned to Simon and spoke with great feeling,

"This has meant much to me, Simon, and I know that it had special meaning for the Messiah as well, and with heartfelt pleasure, I now bequeath it unto you." Matthias then placed the small scroll into Simon's hand and as he gazed into his eyes, the old man said, "You have sought for wealth, my son, and that which I now give unto you is worth more than all the riches in the world. Take it, read it and obey it."

Simon could only nod as he felt his fingers carefully close around the scroll.

Matthias leaned back against the pillows and sighed deeply. "My errand is now complete. I have finished my assigned task. Go, young Simon. Return to Cyrene and your wonderful family. I shall instruct Demetrius to give unto you sufficient money for your passage home." He patted Simon on the arm one last time. "May the God of our fathers guide your journey and bless your life."

Simon reluctantly stood and then bowed before the old merchant. "How shall I ever be able to thank . . ."

Matthias lifted his hand into the air. "No thanks are needed, my son. Go now in peace."

Simon tearfully turned and walked towards the cedar door which he had entered but an hour or so earlier. He turned one last time to gaze upon the great

Matthias. The old man faintly smiled and once again raised his hand, this time in farewell.

"Always remember, my son. You can indeed accomplish any worthy task of your choosing, achieve any noble desire of your heart, rise above the fervent heat of adversity, regardless of its source, and vanquish any foe or challenge that stands before you, if you will but only stay close to your God and never, ever surrender, no matter how enduring the struggle."

Simon gratefully nodded. "I shall remember, most noble Matthias." He then quietly exited the room, shutting the door behind him. Never would he see the great merchant again.

Chapter Thirteen

Simon stood on the deck of the Phoenician freighter looking out over the Great Sea. There was a gentle breeze blowing from the north and the sky was clear. The sun's warming rays felt good on his face. He would arrive in Cyrene in two days.

As he gazed at the beauty of the azure sky, Simon's thoughts turned to Matthias and he wondered if the great merchant had finally returned home to his family and his God. He reached into the small, leather bag which hung at his side and with great care he removed the scroll which Matthias had given to him. He opened it with trembling hands and began to read. . . .

The Words Of The Sacred Scroll

Have no fear, and let thy doubts fall from thee, for it is I, your Creator. Your Eternal Father. He who dwells in the heavenly courts above. He who governs all things, who knows all things and who controls the universe and all things that exist therein. For have I not created all things? Do they not come forth at my command? Are they not mine?

Yea, in the beginning, I created the heavens and the earth. And I moved upon the waters amidst the darkness that covered the earth, and I commanded that there should be light. And was not my voice obeyed?

I commanded the waters to be gathered together unto one place, that the dry land may appear. And was this not so?

Yea verily, I commanded the earth to bring forth grass, the herb yielding seed, and all manner of trees and vegetation. And is not the earth filled with such things?

And I God commanded the greater light to rule the day and the lesser light to rule the night. Does not the sun shine forth its brilliant light during the day, and the moon provide light during the night?

I created every living creature upon the face of the earth, both in the sea and on the land, and I did command the beasts and the fowls to multiply and replenish the earth. And is not the land and sea filled with all manner of life?

I God then looked upon the earth and all things that were thereon and was pleased, yet even amidst all the splendor of my creative hand, I had not yet conceived my greatest miracle.

For it is you! You are my most precious creation! For what is of greater importance to a loving father than his wondrous children? Yea, there is none other who is capable of loving thee as I do, nor caring as I care for thee, or feeling as I feel for thee.

It was with great joy that I witnessed thy birth into mortality. I rejoiced in the newness of thy life and reveled in thy innocence and purity. I wept tears of happiness as you breathed your first mortal breath, and laughed within myself as you took thy first steps. It is true . . . I laugh, I cry, I smile, I worry, I rejoice, I love, all for thee.

Yea, many times have I witnessed thy tears as you cry in the darkness of the night, and I have beheld the breaking of thy heart as you face challenges and trials along the path of life. You wonder how a loving father could allow you to face such adversity.

And yet, just as many before you, you have failed to understand; yea, you have failed to comprehend the work and glory of a loving Creator. For if you did understand my glorious purposes, then never would you have cursed such burdens and obstacles, rather you would have fallen upon thy knees, sending thy prayers heavenward and given mighty thanks for the trials which you are called to endure. For surely there exists a grand purpose for such challenges, and much good shall flow unto thee because of them.

Yea, imagine a formless block of stone which stands before an artist. To many, it is nothing more than a worthless piece of marble, but to the creator, to the sculptor, its value is priceless. For as he gazes upon the lifeless stone, only he can envision and see the beauty which lies therein, and only he knows how to work the roughened and shapeless rock until the noble figure is formed. Such a work, however, is not easily accomplished and requires much patience and time. It is surely an arduous task, but is indeed well worth the hardship that must be borne.

Like the stone, you also possess within thyself a noble figure. It is true! You are my greatest miracle! Behold the beauty and the majesty of all that surrounds thee. Yea, behold the lilies of the field, the great mountains, the mighty rivers, the stars in the firmament that blanket the heavens, and all else which I have created; yet even amidst all their splendor and grandeur, they pale in comparison to thee!

Perhaps others do not behold thy greatness, and perhaps it has even escaped thy view, but it has not escaped mine. I know what lies deep within thy precious soul, and I know better than any other what is necessary to form and free thy noble self.

But just as the beauty of a pearl is created through hardship and toil, and the steel of a brave warrior's sword is hardened for battle by exposure to intense heat, so also the splendor of thy noble self is forged best with the flames of adversity and challenge.

Oh, how I wish that I could rid thee of all human strife, physical pain, mental anguish, adversity and trial; thus allowing thee to bask continually in the warming rays of peace, security and comfort.

But if I were to do so, then I would be doing thee a most terrible injustice, for if I were to entirely seal the portals of sorrow, challenge and hardship from thee, then I would be excluding from thy life thy most prized teachers. For such trials can indeed be valued benefactors as you acquire from them patience, knowledge, faith, perseverance, humility, long-suffering, self-mastery, and strength of character. For it is by facing and overcoming the obstacles and trials of life that you shall gain the noble rewards which you seek in this world, and of greater importance,

91

in the eternal realm yet to come. For this very reason, there must exist times of trial and challenge, times of refinement, times of learning.

The key then becomes, how shall you face such challenges? Yea, will you abandon the fight when the battle becomes difficult, or will you struggle on at all costs? Will you back away and shudder when you face the fervent heat of adversity, or will you strive with all thy might to pass through its intense flames? Will you allow despair to overcome thee and dam thy earthly and eternal progress, or will you rise above such feelings? Will you ignorantly curse the very experiences which will in time forge for thee the strong character needed to climb the mountains of life, or will you learn and grow from them?

Do you not see that my only desire and glory is for thee to achieve that which is rightfully yours; yea, to become thy greatest and most noble self? And do you not now see that it is by enduring and conquering the trials and obstacles of this life that will make possible such a grand and glorious destiny?

But remember and never forget; do not allow adversity and challenge to destroy thy soul and peace of mind. Never give into them. Never! Endure them, for they shall last but as the blink of an eye. Yea, struggle against them and rise above them, and in time you shall be victorious!

Always know of my deep love and compassion for thee, and know that it is my desire to strengthen thee in thy moment of trial and adversity. It is, therefore, with a tender heart that I bequeath unto thee this heavenly gift, "The Divine Covenant." Keep it sacred and hold it nigh unto thee all the days of thy life. When you rise in the morning, let it be the first words which enter thy soul and grace thy mind. Yea, let not a single day pass without commencing thy labors by reading its sacred commands.

If you are faithful to this charge, and obey the divine instructions found herein, then you shall witness mighty miracles in thy life, changes in thy soul that you once thought impossible. In time, you shall possess the understanding, the power and the inspiration needed to face and overcome any challenge or trial, no matter how fervent its heat, and by so doing, you shall indeed stand supreme and victorious in the battle of life!

The Divine Covenant

I must confess that it is so. I have, at times, abandoned the fight. There have indeed been moments when I have shuddered and cowered before the intense heat of adversity. I have often allowed despair to drag me down to the dredges of self-pity, and I have surrendered my soul to the obstacles and trials of life.

But never again! That was yesterday, and yesterday lies buried beneath the sands of time. I shall waste no further thought upon it, and I now covenant to remember it no more.

Today dawns a new beginning, a season of rebirth. As I greet this glorious morn, I rejoice that I am blessed with yet another day of life. For it is a day filled with endless opportunity. A day to love, a day to laugh, a day to labor, a day to succeed. It is a day to face and defeat adversity. A day to be victorious.

My heart beats with renewed passion. My breath is strong. My resolve and will are refreshed and fortified. Like a trained warrior I am prepared to fight and meet the challenges and opportunities which await me.

And just as I have covenanted to forget the ills of the past, I also promise that I shall no longer forsake the opportunities of today for the morrow, for now I realize this important secret: tomorrow never comes, it is always today. Today is here. There is not, nor ever shall be, another like it. I, therefore, covenant to live it to the fullest.

If there be an appointed time to work, then I shall labor like none other before me. If there be time to love, then I shall love with all my heart and soul. If there be time to serve my fellow man, then I shall serve him as if he were my God. If there be time to play and laugh, then I shall enjoy this time just as a little child. And if this be a day of rest, then I shall rest from my labors, remembering that even God rested the seventh day.

I covenant here and now that I shall be strong if I am called upon to face challenges and trials this day. If they be mild, then I shall rejoice, but if they be extreme, then I shall rejoice even greater. For if I curse my opportunities and trials, then I but curse my teachers and my counselors. Them I shall no longer curse. Rather, I shall be humble and patient, and I shall learn the heaven-sent wisdom they would share with me. Their taste, at first, may be bitter, but in time they shall allow me to savor the sweetness of life.

But regardless of what I am called to bear, I shall never allow it to disturb my peace of mind. Never again shall adversity defeat me. Never again will I surrender my soul to it.

If discouragement comes my way, then I shall count my blessings and continue the battle. Yea, I shall number my blessings each one individually, and I shall regard and treasure them for what they truly are; divine gifts from a loving God. I shall never again revere them as anything less, and daily, in the deepest of humility, shall I thank He

94

who is the spring from which all my blessings flow. By so doing, I shall learn this great lesson: I am indeed a rich and blessed person!

And always, regardless of my station in life, I shall endeavor to uplift, inspire and serve those who are less fortunate than myself. Yea, I shall seek out the hungry to feed them, the naked to clothe them, the lonely to befriend them, the ill to comfort them and the broken-hearted to encourage them.

For by losing myself in the service of others, a great miracle shall occur in my life: yea, the sorrows of my heart and the trials of my soul shall diminish until they are as but a feather upon my back; their yoke having been made easy and their burdens light by He who is always mindful of me.

I further covenant that I shall greet every person I meet with a cheerful countenance and a warm smile. No longer shall I harbor feelings of ill will or malice for another, and no longer shall I permit the venom of hate and envy to poison my soul and peace of mind. Instead, I covenant to forgive, to love, to support, to serve and to applaud. I can either destroy or build; I covenant to build.

I also covenant to fortify my soul against moments of adversity and trial by nurturing it with that which will edify my being and help me to feel uplifted, positive, unconquerable, motivated and inspired. Yea, I shall behold the setting sun and bask in its majesty. I shall gaze upon the stars and absorb their tranquillity. I shall search out the beauty of the earth and enjoy its splendor. I shall pause to laugh at the humor which surrounds me. I shall read the uplifting word and surge with its motivation, and I shall listen to music which inspires my soul. Yea, I shall take advantage of such heaven-sent gifts, and I shall feast upon them daily. In time, there beauty, inspiration and richness shall permeate and empower my entire being.

And above all, I covenant that if I am called upon to pass through the raging inferno of life; yea, if the fierce tempests of illness, death, challenge and despair become mine enemy; if the skies become darkened, and all the elements of earth combine against me; and above all, if the very portals of hell shall swing open wide after me, I shall never give up! Not ever! I shall press on with faith, valor and passion, with my God by my side.

Yea, daily shall I rend the heavens with my prayers, supplicating Him to sustain me, comfort me and uphold me. For is there any mightier than He? And does He not implore me to knock, that He might answer? Yea, does He not bid me to seek after Him, that I may drink deeply from the well of His strength, hope, peace, compassion and wisdom?

For is there an aching heart to be found that He will not comfort, or a tear that He cannot dry with the garment of His infinite love? Yea, is there a troubled spirit that He will not lift, or a discouraged soul that He cannot inspire?

Does there exist a problem in the grand expanse of creation that He is not able to solve? Is there a river too swift for Him to ford, or a mountain too high and perilous for Him to climb?

Yea, verily, He is God almighty, my Eternal Father! There is nothing in all the universe which lies beyond the breadth of His great power. Thus, if He be with me, then it matters little what is against me. For there exists no worthy trial, challenge or task that any two beings cannot endure, overcome or accomplish so long as one of them is He who dwells in the kingdoms above!

But though He can move great mountains and stop raging rivers with but a simple command from His lips, I shall not ask that He remove the peaks which I encounter along my path, rather I shall plead only for His divine assistance in climbing them. But let there be no mistake; it is I who must climb them!

Yet of this I am certain; my Father will never forsake me! For truly, as He has proclaimed, I am His greatest miracle! And during those times when I can climb no farther, having given my all, I know that He will carry me to the summit of the mountains of life on the wings of His everlasting love.

Today, blessed with His sustaining power, I shall fight the good fight. I shall bear the crosses of life with my head held high, forever trusting in a loving and all-knowing God. I shall never retreat. I shall always move forward, even if it means that I must crawl upon my knees for a time.

I shall endure. I shall keep the faith. I shall rest when needed, but I shall never give up. Never! I shall rise every time I fall. I shall gasp for every breath if I must, but I shall overcome. And in time, I shall win and wear the crown of the victor!

For I can indeed accomplish any worthy task of my choosing, achieve any noble desire of my heart, rise above the fervent heat of adversity, regardless of its source, and vanquish any foe or challenge that stands before me, if I will but only stay close to my God and never, ever surrender, no matter how enduring the struggle!

Today is to be enjoyed and savored. It is a new day. It is my day. It is a gift from God. And how I make use of this precious gift is, in return, my gift back to Him. I shall, therefore, make this day the greatest gift of all! It shall be a day filled with love, passion, service, gratitude, laughter and, yes, perhaps even tears. But it shall be my day, and it will be the greatest day of my life! Such is my promise and so it shall be!

Chapter Fourteen

Simon slowly rose from the mahogany lounge where he had been sitting with Rachel and turned towards the direction of the house. The sun had set and the evening air blowing in from the Great Sea was turning cold. Rachel did not follow, for she knew of her husband's destination and understood his desire for solitude.

In moments, Simon entered their bed chamber and made his way to a small cedar chest positioned in the corner of the room. He removed the lock which held the sacred contents secure, and after opening the chest, Simon carefully and with much reverence withdrew the small scroll he had received from Matthias some thirty years earlier.

Just as instructed, Simon had read the divine message every morning since his return to Cyrene, and it had miraculously changed his life. The great transformation, however, did not occur with ease to be sure, for it took effort, courage, perseverance and discipline, but with the passing of time, Simon had come to better understand his adversities and trials. He was then determined never again to permit such challenges to hold him back, and with the help of his God, he did not allow it.

Every morning after reading the scroll, Simon vowed that he would obey The Divine Covenant without deviation. As he departed his home for the labors of the day, he promised himself that he would not return until his appointed time. He would toil on, carrying a song in his heart to encourage his soul. No longer would the gulls see his disheartened face.

Whenever he knocked on a door or met a customer in the marketplace, he would instantly extend his hand and warmly smile while greeting the person with a kind salutation. At first, such an act was terribly difficult, but in time, Simon noticed a small miracle; soon people seemed not to notice his disfigured face, and if they did, it seemed of little importance. Instead, they noticed the change in his spirit and in his heart, and with the passing of time, the people actually looked forward to Simon's visits and were genuinely disappointed when his daily schedule did not include their area of the city.

Within a few years, Simon became one of the most successful merchants in all of Cyrene, but of greater importance, he was a man highly honored and much beloved by his people. Often they would come to him for assistance, a comforting word or advice. And never did Simon turn anyone away when he was in a position to offer assistance.

Many times, parents would awaken in the early hours of the morning to find bounteous supplies of food and clothing at their doors. Birthday gifts were miraculously delivered, bills paid, charitable acts performed and hearts touched in times of despair, and although the people of the city suspected, they never knew for certain the true identity of their kind benefactor.

Oh there were days of discouragement to be sure, but during such times of challenge and heartache, Simon would always turn his thoughts back to the knoll where he had carried the Savior's cross, to the garden tomb where the miracle of all miracles had taken place and to his interview with the great merchant, Matthias. Such precious memories, along with the divine and inspiring words of the scroll always helped to put life's trials and challenges into their proper perspective. Never again would he curse them, but never again would they defeat him, no matter how difficult and enduring the fight.

Simon sat on the bed and gazed upon the wondrous scroll. He then reached back and felt the large scar which crossed his shoulders, the one he had suffered while bearing the Savior's cross. He considered both as cherished treasures, and he honestly could not say which he valued the most.

It was then that Simon's most trusted steward, Jeremiah, entered the room and bowed. "Forgive the intrusion, sire, but a man from Jerusalem desires to speak with you. He insists that it is urgent business."

Simon looked curiously at his servant. "Does he travel alone?"

"He claims to have left his small party at the port here in Cyrene. No one is with him at this time."

Simon nodded. "Very well, good friend. Permit his entrance and show him to the western porch. See to it that he is given food and wine to refresh himself. I shall meet with him there."

Once again Jeremiah bowed his head. "It shall be done, sire."

Simon then carefully returned the scroll to the chest and locked it. As he made his way to the western porch, he hesitated to take care of some business and to allow the traveler ample time to eat his meal.

He was just finishing when Simon walked out onto the porch.

Upon seeing his host, the stranger stood and extended his hand. Simon opened his mouth to speak, but hesitated when he beheld his guest, for there was something most familiar about him. "I bid you a kind welcome to Cyrene," Simon finally said while grasping the man's hand. "Please sit and tell me how I may be of service to you."

"Forgive my unannounced visit, sir, but are you Simon, the great merchant?"

Simon humbly nodded. "I am Simon and I do labor as a merchant here in Cyrene."

"I also understand that you are a faithful follower of Jesus of Nazareth, He who was crucified many years ago in Jerusalem."

Simon cautiously gazed into the eyes of the man who sat before him. He then abruptly stood. "And is the purpose of your visit to bring harm to this household simply because of our beliefs?!"

The stranger, seeing his error, also stood. "No, Simon, no! You misunderstand. I am John, one of His disciples, and come from . . ."

"John?!" interrupted Simon.

The man nodded. "Yes, I am John, an apostle of the Lord."

Simon moved forward, grasped the disciple by the shoulders and stared deeply into his eyes. It was so! The face was now aged and partially covered by a graying beard, but it was indeed the same man Simon had seen on several occasions throughout the week of the race some thirty years ago.

"Forgive me, John," pleaded Simon, motioning to the chair. "Please sit and rest yourself while you tell me of your errand."

"It grieves me to say that I am here asking for your financial assistance, Simon."

Simon only nodded. His eyes revealed his eagerness

101

to help.

"I do not know if you are fully aware of the terrible plight of our people in certain areas of the empire?" questioned John.

"I have heard news that some have been jailed for their convictions of the Messiah," answered Simon.

John slowly shook his head. "If it were only that simple. No Simon, I am afraid that the persecution has intensified to such an extreme that many of our people are suffering terrible atrocities, even death by the cruelest of means."

Simon sat stunned in his chair. "I had no idea that conditions had progressed to such a sorry state."

John nodded and the two men sat without speaking a word.

After a long moment of silence, Simon intently sat up and asked, "Tell me then, John, what may I do to assist my distant brothers and sisters in this most desperate hour?"

"It saddens me to say that many have been forced to live in hiding, and since they cannot labor with their own hands or conduct their normal business affairs, a tremendous amount of money is needed to support them in their time of need. For this reason have I come to you, Simon. You are one of the few believers whose assets have not been confiscated by the Romans."

Simon did not hesitate. He stood, walked to the door and summoned Jeremiah. The servant appeared within seconds.

"Jeremiah, how much wealth is presently in the treasury?" questioned Simon.

Jeremiah looked troubled. "The entire amount, sire?"

"Yes. Everything."

"I have not calculated the figures for several days, but I would estimate that there is easily a million gold talents."

"It is well, my trusted friend. Jeremiah, please

listen to me carefully and do not think to question my commands, even if they seem strange to you, for I have no time to explain."

"As you wish, sire."

"You will take from the treasury one million gold talents . . ."

John abruptly stood to interrupt, "Simon, that is too much for you to . . ."

Simon politely, but authoritatively raised his hand. "Do not concern yourself, John. All shall be well."

The disciple was at first amazed and startled at Simon's forcefulness, but he then realized that this was the merchant's domain and he had apparently settled upon a course of action, a course which could not be stopped. John, therefore, returned to his chair, whereupon Simon continued his orders to Jeremiah.

"Take one million gold talents from the treasury and hide them in bushels of wheat. These are to be loaded onto our freighter and disguised as our normal shipment destined for the many ports which lie along the Great Sea. Do you understand my instructions thus far?"

"Yes, sire."

"Please take ten additional men with you to guard the gold and accompany John wherever he desires to sojourn. You and the men will personally stay with him and his associates until all the gold has been delivered according to his instructions. You will obey him as you would me."

"Yes, sire."

"You will depart as soon as the gold can be loaded. I suppose that such a journey and errand will take two or three months to complete."

"It shall be done, sire," said Jeremiah as he turned to fulfill Simon's commands.

John stood and embraced Simon. "May the God of Heaven bless you for such generosity, my dear friend. I do not know how I shall ever be able to thank you."

"No thanks are needed, John, for it is only by the grace of God that I am even in a position to offer such assistance. Besides, what value is there to the blessing of wealth if it is not used for the benefit of mankind?"

John simply nodded his head. "I understand."

Later that night, as the two men sat watching the splendor of the star-filled sky with Rachel, Simon noticed the disciple's distant gaze. "You seem to be thinking of another place, another time."

After a brief moment, John turned to Simon. "Do I? My sincerest apologies. I am afraid that I am not being very attentive to so gracious a host."

Rachel stood to pour more wine into the visitor's goblet. "Do not concern yourself," she said. "We understand."

John took the gentle wine from Rachel and said, "My thoughts are so easily turned on a night such as this for it reminds me of something that I wish I could share with our fellow believers; something that would indeed help them during such times of hardship and struggle."

"What is it, John? If it be so valuable, perhaps there is a means of obtaining it," offered Simon.

"I am afraid that such is an impossibility, my dear friend, even for someone as you. For that which I speak of has been lost to the sands of time for many years now."

"Tell us of it," said Rachel as she sat next to Simon, tenderly grasping his hand.

John sighed deeply and looked up at the stars. "It was on many nights such as this that Jesus often sought solitude so that He might meditate and pray. Towards the end of His life, He invited us, meaning His disciples, to accompany Him, for it was His desire to strengthen us before His death and departure from this world. I remember those nights so very well, for often He would read a most wondrous and inspiring message from a small scroll."